KUNLUN SAGA

Novel

Sema Shubekabu

Los Angeles

Word Farmers Press

2025

WORD FARMERS PRESS

ISBN: 979-8-9932282-5-9 (Paperback)
ISBN: 979-8-9932282-8-0 (Digital Ebook)

Cover design by: KMS Arafat
Edited by: Robert Sucher

Printed in the United States of America.

CONTENTS

FOREWORD

1.

The year 2049 is coming to an end. Terrible things are happening on Earth and in Heaven. War is raging. But it is not Earthlings who are fighting.

The creatures fighting each other have been battling on our planet for several days now. They are very different from each other. Those who first appeared on Earth arrived from space in large starships. All of their space frigates are black and disc-shaped. The diameter of each of these ships is no less than 5 kilometers. There are so many of them gathered near our planet in space that they block out the stars in the night sky.

These aliens mainly conduct combat operations in small, egg-shaped fighter pods. The pods are no larger than a passenger car. They fly very fast, instantly reaching the speed of light.

The human eye cannot see how these pods move. They are difficult to spot even when stationary because they are translucent and easily change color like a chameleon. These flying machines only become visible when they are shot down.

The weapons of the pods have enormous destructive power. The laser cannons can fire rapid bursts, turning everything into burning ash. The electromagnetic bombs they drop leave kilometer-long craters.

The warriors flying these deadly machines wear skintight black spacesuits that cover their entire bodies. The spacesuits are made of a material that looks very much like smooth black plastic and provide their wearers with reliable protection, as ordinary bullets cannot even scratch this material.

Turbines are located on their forearms and soles, allowing the wearers to take off and move freely both in the air and underwater. This allows warriors to leave their fighters even during flight.

When the aliens land and begin clearing the area of survivors and those who continue to resist, their autopiloted aircraft hover above them, providing fire support from the air and tracking enemy movements. After completing the operation, the alien warriors return to their pods.

2.

These creatures resemble humans in appearance, but their body proportions are very different from those of humans: their torso, arms, and legs are very short, while their head is disproportionately large and oval-shaped. Its length makes up about one-third of the entire body, and its diameter is slightly less than the width of the shoulders. They have virtually no neck and are much shorter than humans: even the tallest of them do not exceed 140 cm.

In terms of their movements and behavior, these creatures closely resemble insects. They always stay together and move only in groups. They do this very quickly and in a coordinated manner. These creatures possess tremendous physical strength. Each of them is capable of lifting objects weighing several tons off the ground, smashing concrete walls to smithereens, and punching through the door of an armored vehicle with a single blow.

They are most likely either cyborgs or robots. This is because very often during battle, a box instantly flies up to the wounded insectoid, from which mechanical tentacles extend and begin to mend the injured creature. Usually, this flying ambulance simply replaces damaged body parts with new ones. It does this in a fraction of a second. The only way to fail to save a cyborg warrior is if he has suffered a serious head injury, which, however, was very rare during battles with earthlings.

3.

With such technical and tactical superiority, these demons wiped out the Earth's population like grass. Those who survived are kept in concentration camps. Occasionally, some prisoners manage to escape and hide in the mountains or underground.

Having destroyed the armies of countries that tried to resist them, these little black monsters began to extract minerals from the Earth. They pumped out everything from the ground that could give them energy. They did this on a huge scale, which led to natural disasters. Earthquakes began. Volcanoes awoke. And later, tsunamis several kilometers high crashed into the continents one after another.

This did not stop the insectoids. When the elements calmed down and the storms subsided, they continued to extract energy resources from the earth. As a result, most of the flora and fauna died. The process of photosynthesis was disrupted. The world's oceans began to shrink dramatically. Due to the lack of oxygen in the atmosphere, it became very difficult to breathe.

Now these insect-like people siphon the Sun's energy using huge extractor beams. Instead of the yellow ball that warmed our planet and brought a new bright day, now a white ball, somewhat resembling the Moon, rises in the east every morning. This bleaching disk, still shines, but hardly warms us. If the insectoids do not stop, our sun will soon go out completely.

Most of the land surface is now covered only by deserts, ruined cities buried in sand, and huge ice floes. Eternal winter reigns everywhere. Darkness has enveloped what was once a blue and vibrant planet.

With the start of new fighting, the dead silence is broken by the whistling of shells, deafening explosions, and heart-rending, inhuman screams. It is very cold and terrifying.

4.

Those who fight against the insectoids appeared on Earth just a few days ago. This happened when all life on the planet had been almost completely destroyed. They came out of nowhere, unexpectedly and swiftly attacking the enemy.

A bright silver light emanates from each of them. It is very dazzling, so it is impossible to see these warriors clearly. All that can be said about their appearance is that they are indistinguishable from humans.

These glowing silhouettes move very quickly, like flashes of lightning. They can jump great heights and distances. These silhouettes can fly, disappear unexpectedly, and reappear. They calmly pass through any solid objects, be they walls, rocks, or trees.

They fight without weapons, using only their hands, foreheads, and stomachs to emit powerful electromagnetic discharges capable of striking enemies from a great distance. These glowing silhouettes can destroy their enemies by shooting laser-like beams from their eyes.

Several glowing warriors standing next to each other and emitting wave-like light from their eyes can create a huge spinning laser funnel and direct it at the enemy. Several hundred meters high, this rotating laser tornado burns everything in its path, leaving not even ashes behind. Insectoids, their ships, aircraft, military equipment, and the structures they have built are instantly burned when caught in this vortex.

Although they are fewer in number, they significantly surpass their enemies in strength. Insectoid warriors often suffer losses in battles with them, but their ranks are invariably replenished after a while.

When the number of dead and wounded little black soldiers reaches critical levels, and new forces have not yet arrived on the battlefield, the remaining pod pilots become combat-ready fighters ejecting from their planes and continue the battle on the ground. Meanwhile, their pods are scattered into tiny particles, turning into a dust cloud. Heated to extremely high temperatures, they begin to hover in the air like a giant swarms of wasps, burning everything they touch, while bypassing their black soldiers and causing them no harm. If necessary, pods can reassemble from this dust cloud in an instant to retrieve their soldiers from the battlefield.

The only way to stop the fiery swarm and the reinforcements arriving during battle for glowing ones is to blow themselves up. The explosion of a single glowing warrior destroys millions of insect-like monsters and clears the Earth of hot dust clouds.

In one of the battles that took place near where we are being held, I saw the glowing ones penetrate the black suits of the insect-people and burn them from the inside. As they burned alive, the insect-people let out ghastly screams.

Unlike the insectoids, the glowing ones do not bother humans, but they do not interact with them either. They communicate very little among themselves. As a rule, they exchange short phrases during battle. Their language is very similar to Cantonese. Although most likely, it just seemed that way to me. I am quite old, my hearing is spotty.

5.

The insectoids keep me in a common barracks with the other elderly prisoners. These creatures don't bother us much. The younger prisoners are less fortunate. They are subjected to horrific experiments and all kinds of torture.

I know I won't last long in these barracks, but I'm only worried about my son and grandchildren. After the insectoids attacked Earth, I haven't seen Tim or his little ones since.

Once, a prisoner who arrived at the camp after me told me how he had seen a man who could crush insectoids with a single shout. When I heard this, I realized he was talking about my son. It seemed that he was no longer hiding his gift and had decided to openly fight back against the black soldiers.

Now it's pointless for me to be afraid that someone will find out about his superpowers. Circumstances have changed. Although I must admit, I've lived my whole life in fear that someone would find out about it...

Part 1 Secrets of Kunlun Mountain

Chapter 1 Unexcepted Arrival

1.

When Alexei was still very young, he arrived in China with burning eyes and a firm intention to learn Chinese. At that time, when the country's economy was booming, Putonghua — the official language — was in high demand. Students, businessmen, dreamers from every corner of the world were heading to China to study, work, or simply catch a glimpse of a land that had been closed to foreigners for so long.

He flew into Beijing in early September 2000. The sky was cloudless, the streets blazing with heat. It felt strange: just last evening in Moscow, he had walked through cold rain, his coat heavy on his shoulders.

After traveling around for a while, Alexei enrolled in Chinese language courses at a college in Qingdao. He liked the city right away. The sea was close, the food was cheap and delicious, and the locals welcomed him with open friendliness. It was a good place to begin.

Classes started early in the morning and ended after lunch. His group had about twenty students, most of them from South Korea, with just a handful from Europe and America. Despite the mix, the atmosphere was always warm, and they spoke only Putonghua to each other.

One day, during introductions, a girl's clear voice carried across the classroom:

"My name is Nicole. I was born and raised in San Francisco. My parents are from Guangdong Province. They met in America, got married, and stayed after my father found work with a Chinese company. I've been studying Putonghua here in Qingdao for several months."

She spoke fluently, though her soft southern accent slipped through whenever she tried to pronounce "sh." Alexei listened closely, fascinated. If she hadn't mentioned her American upbringing, he might have thought she'd grown up in Guangdong itself.

Nicole smiled as she continued: "At home, we only speak Cantonese. Putonghua came later, after I arrived here. The hardest part for me is the characters — so many, and all different! But I love the food here: braised eggplant, chicken skewers, potato strips with chili. Even rice tastes better in China. I like Chinese food. I love braised eggplant, chicken skewers, and potato strips with red chili peppers. Here in China, I've grown to love eating rice. It tastes much better here."

Her laughter was quick and bright, and Alexei found himself listening more intently than to anyone else.

After a few weeks, he finally gathered the courage to talk to her after class.

"I haven't seen you for almost two weeks. Were you sick?"

"Yes, I caught a cold," she replied with a little shrug.

"How can you catch a cold in a city where it's always summer?"

She laughed, her eyes lighting up. "Maybe too much ice cream. There's this green tea popsicle — I'm addicted. Have you tried it?"

Whenever Nicole stumbled in Chinese, she slipped into English. Seeing that Alexei didn't understand, she began showing him translations on her electronic dictionary. Slowly, their conversations grew easier. Soon, she was sending him daily text messages in Chinese.

For Alexei, each reply was an effort: deciphering unknown characters, flipping through his dictionary, piecing together sentences. At first, it was frustrating, but over time his vocabulary grew, and their messages became longer and warmer.

Friendship turned into hours of talking after class, shared homework, study sessions for exams. On weekends, they laughed at Hollywood movies dubbed into Chinese and strolled along the beach, their feet sinking into hot sand. They were young, curious, and inseparable.

By the end of the school year, friendship had become love. Nicole was supposed to return to America for the summer, but at the last minute, she decided to stay. One evening, as they sat on a bench by the sea, Alexei noticed her silence. She brushed off his jokes, her gaze distant.

"Something happened." she whispered suddenly, her dark eyes clouded.

"怎么回事儿?[1]" Alexei asked cheerfully.

Tears welled up and spilled down her cheeks before she could answer. Finally, in a trembling voice, she confessed:

"I'm pregnant... If my father finds out, I'll have to..." Her words broke. "I must have an abortion."

Alexei's mind froze. He tried to reassure her, promising he wouldn't abandon her. That same evening, he found a private clinic online and convinced her to go. But the doctor, after examining Nicole, shook his head. Speaking slowly so she could catch the words, he explained:

---

[1] zěnme huíshìr? – "What happened?" (transcription and translation from Chinese)

"This girl is in very poor health. If she terminates the pregnancy, she will likely never bear children again. And I cannot risk her life for this procedure."

2.

Nicole didn't dare tell her parents. She avoided trips home, offering excuses, and when they called, she only showed her face on video. The rest she kept hidden.

Pregnancy weighed on her heavily. Restless nights, mood swings, irritation at the smallest things. Friends drifted away. She studied harder than ever, but outside class she seemed withdrawn.

When her son was born prematurely at seven months, it was nothing short of a miracle that he survived.

The dormitory refused to house a family with a baby, so Alexei searched desperately until he found an elderly landlady, Zhang Lin, renting a modest two-room apartment near the college.

Zhang Lin, widowed and childless, lived one floor above them. She had spent her life trading real estate and now kept several apartments for rent. But more than the money, she seemed to crave company. Students brought life into her building, filling it with laughter, quarrels, and music. When summer came and they left, silence returned like a shadow.

For Alexei and Nicole, she became a grandmotherly figure. She watched their son when they were busy, invited them for lunch, and doted on the child with quiet affection.

Nicole's health declined sharply after giving birth. She lost her milk early and had to rely on expensive formulas and medication. Alexei worked relentlessly — as a translator in a travel agency, part-time in a logistics company, tutoring Russian to local students. Still, money was never enough.

Arguments filled the apartment.

"You work every day, yet we still have to count every penny," Nicole snapped one evening.

"And why is that?" Alexei shot back. "Because the lights are on all night! Because of your restaurant orders! We could live more modestly."

Her bitter laugh cut through him. The baby cried, neighbors banged on the walls, and Nicole locked herself in the bedroom while Alexei stood helpless in the kitchen. Only Zhang Lin could calm the child, rocking him gently until silence returned, broken only by Nicole's muffled sobs from behind the bedroom door.

3.

"Let's tell our parents everything. We can't handle this alone," Alexei suggested one night.

"Are you insane?" Nicole's eyes flashed. "My father would never accept me with a child born out of wedlock."

"Then let's get married. Come to Russia. My parents will be happy."

She stared at him, then burst into harsh laughter. "Marry you? A bum who can't even provide for himself? I always knew you were poor. Move to Russia? Never."

Her words struck deep, but Alexei said nothing. She was right — he had failed so many times before. And yet, he clung to one hope: that mastering Chinese would be the key to a different life, a better one.

Late at night, unable to sleep, he wandered into the kitchen. Nicole's books still lay scattered across the table. He picked one up and flipped through it absentmindedly until a photograph caught his eye: soldiers of the Terracotta Army, unearthed by a farmer in 1974.

The article beneath spoke of the first emperor, Qin Shi Huangdi, and the legendary treasures said to be buried in his tomb.

Alexei stared at the page, a quiet thought forming:

If only I could find treasures like that.

Chapter 2 The Beginning of the Treasure Hunt

1.

Gradually, the thought of treasures completely consumed Alexei. Dreaming of hidden riches, he began to ponder where else in China one might find treasures that no one even suspected existed. Which emperors' tombs were still waiting to be discovered?

In his spare time, Alexei read everything he could find on the Internet about treasure hunting. Once, he stumbled upon an article about German businessman Heinrich Schliemann. In his time, Schliemann discovered the city of Troy, whose existence many did not believe in, considering it a myth from Homer's Iliad. Schliemann, who had been fascinated by ancient Greek literature since childhood, insisted that Troy was not a figment of the imagination. So, in the spring of 1873, this German amateur archaeologist made his greatest discovery.

Schliemann's discovery of several ancient Greek cities further strengthened Alexei's intention to search for treasure. Chinese history spanned more than a thousand years, and he knew for certain that there were still many treasures to be found in these lands. He just needed to decide what to look for.

Alexei reasoned as follows: the closer history is to the present day, the fewer secrets and mysteries it holds, which reduces the chances of new discoveries. Therefore, he decided to focus on the history of Ancient China, specifically its rulers.

Looking through the long list of great emperors, he noticed that the first ten of them were mythical heroes. The existence of these ancient rulers was known only from legends and fairy tales. No archaeological evidence confirming the real existence of these kings had been found. This prompted him to follow Schliemann's example and search for information about history in literature, reading Chinese epics and ancient legends.

2.

One of the oldest Chinese collections of legends and tales was the book Shan Hai Jing[2]. Most of the myths about the ancient rulers of China were preserved in this thick book.

It is not known for certain when it was written. Historians believed that it was started around the 5th century BC. Alexei stubbornly ignored the fact that scientists unanimously considered everything described in this book to be nothing more than fiction.

Rereading ancient texts from the Shanhaijing, he tried to find at least some connection between the tales described in them and the real world. Thus, on a modern map of China, Alexei easily found Mount Kunlun. This mountain was mentioned in one of the myths as the place where the Yellow Emperor lived. This figure, who was neither human nor demigod, was known to all Chinese people as Huangdi. The texts described his numerous exploits and discoveries. In them, he was presented as a healer and skilled warrior, a wise ruler, and the greatest inventor. It was believed that this mythical hero gave rise to the entire Chinese nation.

According to one legend, the Yellow Emperor built an entire jade city on Mount Kunlun. This tale mentions that the place in the mountains where Huangdi lived was the source of several rivers.

Looking at the map, Alexei discovered that the only river originating in that region was the Yellow River. However, Mount

---

[2] The Book of Mountains and Seas is an ancient Chinese treatise describing the real and mythical geography of China and neighboring lands, as well as the creatures that inhabit them. (Author's note)

Kunlun itself was located slightly further away from the source of this enormous river. This was clearly visible on satellite maps.

Most likely, Kunlun in the legend is a generalized name for all the mountain ranges in those places. The source of the Yellow River is a more precise reference point. In addition, geographers claim that the source of the Yellow River never changes its location. Perhaps ancient people called the mountain at the source Kunlun? And over time, this name was transferred to another mountain range further away from the source?" wondered the gold-seeking student.

The source of the Yellow River was clearly marked on the map. Alexei even found several settlements nearby that were easy to reach. As it turned out, tourists loved to visit this area. Many wanted to see the place where the great Yellow River began. Something told the young man that this was where he needed to look.

Alexei decided to go there in secret, knowing full well that if anyone found out where he was going, and more importantly, why, they would think he was crazy. Nicole, of course, would also be categorically opposed to this idea and, as always, would make another scene. He was very tired of this, so he left without saying anything to her.

3.

The treasure hunter returned to Qingdao three weeks later without any results. It was the height of summer, and the city was sweltering. The bright sun was blinding. He walked from the train station to his rented apartment. There were few people on the streets. The student campus he passed by was deserted—the holidays had long since begun, and most of the students had gone home.

Alexei imagined how difficult the conversation with Nicole would be and what a scene she would make. The mere thought of it made him feel uneasy. All the way on the train, he racked his brains trying to figure out how to explain his disappearance to her.

But it didn't come to that. The apartment where they lived turned out to be completely empty. All their belongings seemed to have vanished. It was as if Nicole and Tim had never lived there.

He immediately rushed to Zhang's place and heard the baby's hearty laughter as soon as he reached her door. The old woman herself opened the door, holding Tim in her arms.

"Where have you been?" she grumbled unhappily, letting him into the doorway. Alexei stood silently in the hallway, not daring to look her in the eye. She handed him the baby, who immediately began to cry.

"Wait, I'll bring your things," she said and left.

The inexperienced father tried to calm Tim down, but he started crying even louder. After a while, Zhang reappeared in the hallway. She was struggling to drag a large suitcase on wheels belonging to Alexei, which he had bought last summer in Shanghai. The luggage was so full that it was impossible to close the zipper completely.

"Where is Nicole?" he finally decided to ask. The old woman did not answer. Placing the suitcase at the doorstep, she took the child from him and went back into the other room. After a while, she returned and handed him a note from Nicole. It was written in English:

"Alex,

I can't imagine where you've gone. I'm flying home and I'm never coming back here. I'm leaving the baby. I didn't want this child and I still don't. I asked Zhang to look after him until you return. Maybe I lied, because I don't know if you'll ever show up here again. I realized that I never loved you and don't want to tie my life to you and this baby.

Goodbye."

At that moment, Alexei was very confused. Sitting on the floor next to his suitcase in the dark hallway of Zhang's apartment, he wondered what to do next. He had almost no money. He had no idea what to do next, especially with a child in his arms. The only thing that came to mind was to try to persuade the landlady to let Tim stay with her until he found a new place to live and a job.

Grandma Zhang took pity on him and agreed to take the child in for a while. She even allowed the poor guy to stay in the rented apartment until she found new tenants.

Alexei felt a void in his heart. He didn't blame Nicole. It was just that life had once again shown him how illusory his ideas about sincerity, friendship, and love were.

During that long, sleepless night, he couldn't stop thinking that everything would work out if he found the treasure. This gave him hope. So, at his own risk, he decided to continue searching for the treasure.

4.

The next day, Alexei did not go to look for a job or new accommodation. Instead, he went straight to the train station and bought a ticket to the village of Xu, near which he was looking for the jade city.

In those parts, the hospitable locals always gladly let him stay overnight. They had never seen foreigners before and were interested in talking to him. They fed him generously and even gave him food to take with him.

Alexei got hold of a crowbar and a shovel and spent whole days disappearing into the area around the source of the Yellow River, returning to the village in the evening. After a few weeks, he left with nothing and returned to Qingdao, again asking Zhang Lin to look after the baby, and again went off in search.

This continued until almost the end of autumn. The last time Alexei visited Zhang's apartment, the old woman was very ill. She was lying in bed and hardly ever got up. An unfamiliar woman opened the door for him. As it turned out, she was a distant relative of Grandma Zhang. Her name was Wang Mei.

Wang Mei was about 60 years old. She had gray curly hair. She wore a short black rabbit fur coat, a dark green skirt just below the knees, and black suede boots. On her right hand, she wore a ring with a large burgundy gemstone. She looked very stylish and exuded the subtle scent of expensive perfume.

Ms. Wang talked with the student for a long time. After praising his Chinese, she began to ask him all about his life in China. During the conversation, she was often interrupted by phone calls. Sometimes she would switch her attention to Tim and start playing with him, and then, remembering Alexei, she would return to the conversation. She spoke very slowly and politely. She had a constant smile on her face. Her voice was low with a slight hoarseness.

"Grandma Zhang is currently being cared for by a nurse. But it's not very convenient to look after sick people at home, so I decided to transfer her to the hospital. I racked my brains for a long time trying to figure out where Zhang got this baby from. Now I understand everything," Wang continued with a smile.

"Which hospital will she be admitted to? I could help take care of her."

"I don't think that will be necessary. She will be admitted to the central city hospital, where medical staff will look after her around the clock."

Then she looked at Alexei very intently, as if thinking about something, and said:

"You can visit her whenever you want."

After saying this, Wang Mei began to get ready to leave. At the door, she suddenly turned to him and added with the same smile:

"Oh yes, I almost forgot. New tenants will be moving into this apartment soon. You can stay here with the baby until the end of the week, but then you'll have to move out."

During the entire week that Alexei spent at Grandma Zhang's apartment, she didn't say a word and only looked at him sadly when he came into her bedroom. The room smelled strongly of Chinese medicine, and silence reigned. All that could be heard was Grandma's heavy, wheezing breath and the ticking of the wall clock.

The young man sat by her bedside, lost in thought. It seemed impossible to him to continue the search with a child in his arms, but he did not want to give up what he had started. Once again, hoping for the best, he decided to move to the village of Xu with the baby, and early on Sunday morning, after saying goodbye to the old woman, he left Qingdao forever.

5.

After moving to the village with Tim, Alexei began giving private Russian lessons. He held classes in a small hut. In the mornings, it served as a classroom where he taught, and in the evenings, it served as a bedroom for him and Tim.

Alexei was very afraid that he would not be able to cope with the difficulties that fall on the shoulders of young single parents. Tim cried all the time, and his dad could not calm him down. Alexey did not know how to communicate with his child and could not find a way to approach him. At first, the_student was often helped by his neighbors.

But soon everything settled down, and he and Tim began to get along. The child turned out to be very obedient and quick-witted. When Alexei was busy with household chores or teaching classes, his son would quietly play with his toys, draw and color, or simply leaf through children's books.

Alexei gradually began to teach Tim Russian and introduce him to Russian culture: he let him watch cartoons in Russian, listen to Russian songs, and read Russian fairy tales. The boy spoke only Chinese with the locals. Gradually, Tim began to speak two languages.

Caring for Tim filled Alexei's life with meaning and gave him strength. The bitterness of his unrequited love and loneliness dissolved in his son's smile and cheerful laughter.

6.

When the winter cold ended and the snow melted, Alexei began searching for the treasure again, devoting all his free time to it. He dug everywhere: far away in the mountains and near the village.

If there was no one to leave Tim with, he took him along. They often went on expeditions to a small river that started somewhere in the mountains and flowed near their village.

Alexei dug holes no more than a meter in diameter, going as deep as the soil would allow. Finding nothing, he climbed out of the hole and filled it in. Counting a couple of steps from the filled-in spot, he began digging again.

If there was sand in the hole, Alexei didn't fill it in, but made a sandbox for Tim next to it and let him play there. The little boy had toy cars, a shovel, and a bucket to play with. He often started digging holes in his sandbox, imitating his dad.

It was difficult for Alexei not to attract the attention of the peasants with his excavations. There was always someone curious who would pester him with questions about what he was doing. Alexei would laugh it off, replying that he was looking for treasure. Some would laugh in response and wish him luck before continuing on their way, while others would look at him strangely and walk away in silence.

7.

One day during class, several people came to Alexei's house. The woman among them apologized in Chinese and asked if she could attend his lesson. He nodded in response, confused, and continued the lesson.

Those who had entered stood quietly by the front door and watched Alexei teach. When the lesson was over and all the children had left, the same Chinese woman addressed him again, but this time in Russian:

“Hello! My name is Nadia. I studied Russian at Irkutsk University and now work at a local language school. We are in urgent need of Russian teachers. I would like to invite you to work with us.”

As it turned out, representatives of the district administration had come with her. They had heard rumors that a foreigner was working as a teacher in one of the surrounding villages. This aroused their interest, and they decided to visit the village.

Alexei was offered to move to the city and start working at the school Nadia mentioned. Promising to think about it, he wrote down her phone number, and the guests politely said goodbye and left.

After that meeting, Alexei continued his search. However, his enthusiasm gradually began to fade. He thought long and hard about the offer to move to the city and work at a school.

The promise of a good salary and free accommodation in an apartment with all amenities made him wonder for the first time whether it was worth staying in this remote place and searching for something unknown. Digging in the dirt in the cold and heat, especially with a child, seemed crazy to him.

After weighing all the pros and cons, Alexei was increasingly inclined to move. After a week of deliberation, he called Nadia and told her he agreed. Then he bought train tickets, packed his things, and he and Tim set off on their journey.

Chapter 3 The Stone Bell

1.

The city was a few hours away. Tired and desperate, the treasure hunter stared out the window for a long time and reflected on his life. He felt like a loser. Memories flashed before his eyes like trees and houses in a train window. He felt gloomy and sad.

From time to time, he looked away from the window and glanced around. The car was packed with people. It was very noisy. There was a very heavy smell. The luggage racks creaked under the weight of bags, sacks, and suitcases.

People crowded into the aisle and vestibule because they had been unable to buy seats. On weekends and on the eve of holidays in China, this was a common occurrence.

The conductor's booming voice, the loud laughter and conversations of his neighbors, the crying of a child at the end of the car—all this gradually brought Alexei out of his reverie, and he glanced at Tim. His little son was also sitting by the window opposite him. On the floor near the child lay a small aluminum pot filled with various trinkets that had either been given to him or that he had picked up somewhere.

Tim took a toy car, then a spoon, then a plastic cup, then some small pebbles out of the bucket and played with them. Each time he took a new item out of the aluminum container, he put the previous one back. Only one of his toys did he keep with him at all times, hardly ever letting it out of his hands. It was something like a pistachio nut in its shell.

The baby periodically touched various objects around him with this nut: the table, his clothes, a bottle of water, and other things.

After touching an object with the pistachio, he would bring it to his ear and listen carefully, and a moment later he would start laughing happily, and sometimes even squeal with joy.

Alexei became curious about this pistachio that Tim wouldn't part with for a second. His father tried to coax the toy out of his son's hands to get a better look at it, but the boy stubbornly refused to give it up. Then Alexei resorted to trickery and distracted the toddler with a chocolate bar. That's how he managed to get hold of the stone nut for a short time.

2.

It was an oval-shaped pebble. It looked very much like a pistachio shell that was slightly open. Between its two hollow halves, a metal rod was visible: one end protruded slightly outward, while the other was hidden inside, like the rod of a bell.

When Alexei shook the "pistachio," the rod struck its hollow stone halves. "Just like a bell," he confirmed his guess. But the sound it made was barely audible and not particularly melodious. Alexei could only get a good sound when he shook the trinket with all his might.

Alexei couldn't understand why the bell rang so poorly. Its light brown body was smooth and polished to a shine on the outside. The protruding tip of the metal clapper was shaped like a small pyramid.

Looking more closely at the pyramid, Alexei noticed that it consisted of three tiny figures resembling ancient hieroglyphs. The largest of them was attached to the rod and served as the base of the pyramid, the middle one was the central part, and the smallest was the top.

The style of the characters was very similar to jiaguwen — hieroglyphic inscriptions made on turtle shells or ox shoulder blades 1600 BC.

The smallest figure, located at the top, was the prototype of the modern character "上" (shàng), which meant "above." It was attached to the middle figure, which was analogous to the modern character '帝' (dì), translated as "emperor." The third figure, the largest, was attached to the tongue rod and was the ancient ancestor of the character "黄" (huáng), which meant "yellow."

If you read the top and center of the pyramid, it spelled out the word "上帝" (shàng dì), which translates as "God." And if you read the base and center of the pyramid, it spelled out the word '黄帝' (huáng dì), which means "Yellow Emperor."

Alexei's heart was pounding wildly, his throat was dry. Questions swirled in his head: "What is this thing? Did it belong to the Yellow Emperor? How did it end up with Tim, and when? How long have I been unaware of it?"

Chapter 4 The Discovery of the Jade City

1.

Alexei enjoyed working at the school. The obedient and diligent Chinese students picked everything up quickly. It didn't take him long to prepare for classes. The lessons were more like conversations on random topics. He was a spoken language instructor, and all he had to do was speak his native language.

It seemed that his life was back on track, but that stone bell would not leave him alone. He was lost in conjecture as to where Tim could have found it. The only reasonable explanation that came to mind was in one of the sand pits by the river where he used to play in the sand. After working until the end of the school year, he went back to the village of Xu during the summer holidays and resumed his search.

Alexei began digging again along both banks where there was sandy soil. But this time he dug a continuous trench rather than individual holes so as not to miss anything. He dug no more than a meter deep, even though the sandy layer went much deeper.

In one spot, where the stream curved around a rock, the sand layer was no thicker than the length of a shovel blade, and underneath it was something very hard. After clearing this area of sand, Alexei discovered that the hard object he had hit with his shovel was a wide stone step. After clearing it completely, he moved on to the next one, then the third, and so on. Gradually, the entire stone staircase appeared before him. It descended from the river toward a large rock.

After clearing the staircase completely, Alexei was able to get a better look at the stone steps. They were carved from light green jade. Their surface was very even and smooth. All the steps were rectangular in shape, 99 cm long, 66 cm wide, and 8 cm thick.

The staircase descended about five or six meters and ended at a vertical wall carved into the rock. Tapping on the surface of this wall, Alexei discovered a round hole about a meter in diameter. It was located at the very bottom, just above the last step, and was completely filled with sand.

2.

This hole was the entrance to the tunnel. When Alexei had almost completely cleared it of sand, hieroglyphs glowing with yellow light became visible on the walls.

It seemed like it was illumination, and all these hieroglyphs were nothing more than light bulbs powered by electricity. But as soon as the young man touched a hieroglyph or simply held his palm up to it, it immediately disappeared.

The characters were depicted in the Jiaguwen style and resembled those Alexei had seen on the tongue of the stone bell. They covered the entire surface of the tunnel and served as a kind of pattern. It was very pleasing to the eye.

The tunnel was exactly six meters long. Its walls were made of black jade with a perfectly flat and smooth surface. At the end of the tunnel, there was a bright light that grew brighter as Alexei approached.

The moment he reached the end of the tunnel, a bright light blinded him, and he couldn't see anything. His eyes began to sting and water. Squinting, he crawled out by touch, toward the source of the light.

When his eyes adjusted to the bright light and he could see clearly, he saw two dragon statues. They were at least 20 meters tall and made of pure gold. Blue diamonds sparkled in the statues' eyes.

The dragons' mouths were slightly open, revealing their bared teeth. The upper and lower fangs were inlaid with red gemstones and looked as if they were covered in blood.

The dragons towered over the tunnel exit. Like formidable guards, they froze at the moment of attacking the one who dared to disturb the peace of that mysterious abode. Their size was intimidating. It seemed that these two giants were about to crush the man crouching on all fours in front of them.

3.

After catching his breath a bit, Alexei began to look around and noticed a passage leading deeper into the cave. It was a narrow path, partially covered with sand. Its surface was lined with purple jade and ran between the dragon statues.

Passing them, Alexei saw many buildings in front of him, and soon a whole city hidden inside the rock came into view.

In the center stood a huge jade palace with bright yellow walls and a light brown roof. The roof was multi-level — each floor had its own roof. The top floor had a gabled roof — a sharp top and a sloping bottom. The entrance to the palace was decorated with dark red columns with inscriptions in Jiaguwen. As in the tunnel, all the characters glowed with a soft yellow light.

Surrounding the palace were one- and two-story houses with blue roofs and brown walls, also carved from jade. All of them had pointed, curved roofs in the traditional Chinese style, which protruded beyond the walls and were decorated with various animal figures. Many of the houses were almost completely buried in sand, with only the tips of their roofs visible.

There were 12 columns around the perimeter of the city, topped with figures of animals from the Chinese zodiac. The city covered an area of approximately 9 hectares. The entire surface on which it stood was paved with green jade slabs.

The cave reliably protected the buildings from natural disasters and cataclysms. Thanks to this, all the buildings have been preserved in their original form without the slightest damage.

Despite all Alexei's attempts to understand the origin of the dazzling light penetrating every corner of the cave, it remained a mystery to him.

After a while, he felt completely exhausted and decided to continue exploring the jade city the next day. With great difficulty, he made his way to the river, wandered into the village in the dark, and, reaching his hut, fell onto his bed and fell into a death-like sleep.

4.

The next day, Alexei woke up around noon and began to complain that he had woken up so late because he had forgotten to set his alarm clock. When he returned to the steps leading to the tunnel, he saw that a large crowd had gathered there.

It was very lively and noisy. People crowded in line to squeeze through the tunnel into the rock.

As it turned out, early in the morning, one of the villagers was passing by that place and, out of curiosity, looked into the trench dug by Alexei near the river. Discovering steps in it and learning where they led and what was hidden on the other side of the tunnel, he rushed back to the village and told his fellow villagers about everything. Soon, almost all the villagers gathered by the river near the rock to see the jade city with their own eyes.

On the same day, local authorities arrived at the excavation site accompanied by police. After everyone was asked to leave the cave, one of the officials sealed the entrance. He then informed the onlookers that further excavations would be carried out by scientists and that the jade city would only be open to the public once the work was complete.

A couple of days later, the spot on the riverbank where the steps had been found was fenced off with a tall fence. Now you could only get in through a gate. A guardhouse was set up next to it, with a security guard on duty around the clock.

Alexei didn't want to give up so easily. "At the very least, I have the right to free access. And in general, I deserve a reward for discovering the most ancient city in China, and perhaps even in the whole world," he thought to himself.

5.

Every day, the poor soul would come to the site where archaeologists were now conducting excavations and stand at the gate for hours on end.

"Grandfather, let me through," he would sometimes say to the guard.

"I'm not allowed to let anyone in! How many times have I told you that?"

Alexei did not lag behind and after a while approached the booth again to call out to the guard.

"It's not fair to do that! I found this place."

"I'm sorry, I can't let you through."

The security guard, an elderly gentleman, was initially reticent. However, upon learning that Alexei was from Russia, he became more friendly and began to come out of his booth to chat with him.

Lao Yang, as the old man was called, like many other Chinese who lived through the Soviet era, loved Russians very much. He fondly remembered the help Soviet people gave to the Chinese people during difficult times. Grandfather was very familiar with Russian writers and political leaders of the USSR.

He really liked Soviet songs. He demonstrated this many times, singing "Katyusha" and "Not even a whisper can be heard in the garden" in Chinese. After he and Alexei became friends, the old man often asked the young man to sing these songs in Russian.

Lao Yang told his new friend that archaeologists were working inside the rock day and night. They didn't tell him anything about what they had found or seen there. They only came out to get supplies and then went back to work.

During one of these conversations with his grandfather, Alexei suddenly heard Tim's cheerful laughter. As always, he took his son with him if he couldn't find anyone to look after him in the village.

The little boy laughed very strangely. It was neither a laugh nor a squeal. Alexei had never noticed this before.

"Look how he's frolicking in the fresh air. He's squealing with delight!" said Grandpa Lao and laughed.

"Yes! He's the happiest one here," Alexei agreed and began to laugh too.

They approached the spot where the little boy was playing with his toys and began to watch him. All his toys were scattered around him. It was clear that he had long forgotten about them. Sitting on the ground, Tim held his stone pistachio in his hands and never took his eyes off it. Every time it fell out of his hands, he began to squeal with delight. And Alexei and his grandfather couldn't help but laugh again.

Suddenly, the large glass cup with a handle that Grandfather was holding in his hands became covered with cracks.

"I laughed so hard... Didn't burst from laughter myself, but the glass couldn't take it," Lao Yang frowned discontentedly. The child screamed even louder, and the glass vessel shattered into pieces. The grandfather was scalded by the spilled hot tea, and the shards cut his hand, which was holding the glass. He cried out in pain and grabbed his wounded hand.

There was complete silence. Alexei and the old man exchanged glances. Each of them was sure that the glass had burst from the children's screams.

After that incident, Lao Yang stopped coming out of the booth to see Alexei and avoided him in every way possible. Only once, with his arm bandaged, did he tell the student, very irritably but politely, that outsiders were now forbidden to even be near the fence.

After pacing back and forth in front of the gate for a while longer, Alexei realized that he had no chance of getting inside the rock. He had no choice but to return to the city and prepare for the new school year.

The discovery of the Yellow Emperor's jade city brought our gold prospector neither fame nor fortune. What secrets did the temples and palace hide? Was the imperial tomb kept in this ancient city? What treasures and jewels lay there? All these questions remained a mystery to him.

Part 2 An Unusual Child

Chapter 1 Unexplained Phenomena

1.

Alexei continued to work at the school. Since he was at work every day, he had to find a babysitter for Tim. Miss Chen, a Chinese woman, agreed to look after the little boy while he was away from home. She came in the morning and stayed with Tim all day, teaching him preschool arithmetic, drawing, reading, and writing Chinese characters. The child had no time to get bored.

Miss Chen was originally from Guangdong Province and spoke Mandarin with a southern accent. To Alexei's surprise, she communicated with the baby not only in Mandarin, but also in the Cantonese dialect, also known as Yue. His father had no objection, deciding that knowledge of the Cantonese dialect would not be superfluous for the child.

Alexei devoted all his free time to Tim. They walked around the city together, went to the pool, visited the park, and had picnics. As he spent time with the child, Alexei began to notice that the boy was speaking less Russian. This was easy to explain, since he spent most of his time with his nanny. But Alexei tried his best to introduce him to his native culture. He often read Russian fairy tales to Tim, showed him films, and played songs in Russian.

2.

Tim was not a normal child. Alexei became convinced of this when his son was about five years old. One evening, when he came home from work, he found his apartment in complete disarray. The windows, furniture, dishes, and television had been smashed.

Alexei found Miss Chen lying unconscious on the kitchen floor. Blood was flowing from her nose and ears. Tim was kneeling beside her, shaking her shoulder, trying to bring her round. "阿姨! 阿姨!起来! 阿姨起来![3]" he kept repeating. Tears were streaming from his eyes, but he had no bruises or wounds.

The young man immediately called an ambulance and waited for the doctors to arrive. Miss Chen regained consciousness before they came. She looked very frightened and couldn't say a word.

The day after the incident, the local police officer came to Alexei's house and questioned him at length about all the details of what had happened. He also asked Tim a few questions, but the boy stood with his head down and remained silent.

Upon learning which hospital Miss Chen had been taken to, Alexei immediately went to visit her. She looked much better and was already able to speak. He apologized to her for what had happened and asked as delicately as possible what had happened between her and Tim that day.

Miss Chen looked at him fearfully and said quietly:

"It's all my fault."

"What do you mean?"

"That day, the boy wouldn't listen to me at all and didn't want to do his work. He played with his pebble the whole time and acted like he didn't notice me. Finally, I got really angry and snatched the toy out of his hands, saying I wouldn't give it back until he finished all his math and reading assignments. The child froze for a moment, then began to scream hysterically. It was unbearable, and I covered my

---

[3] āyí! āyí! qǐlái! āyí qǐlái! – Auntie! Auntie! Get up, auntie, get up (transcription and translation from Chinese).

ears with my hands. My head hurt badly, as if it were being squeezed in a vice, but he continued. Soon, a mug burst on the desk, and the mirror on the wall was covered with cracks. I don't remember anything else."

Alexei felt uncomfortable after hearing this. Trying to calm her down and explain what had happened, he said:

"It probably happened because the room is very small. The acoustic effect worked like in a speaker."

Chen looked at him strangely, but he continued:

"The sound became so loud that things started to burst."

Chen, not understanding what he was saying, simply replied:

"It's my own fault for bringing the child to this point."

Alexei was unable to console the poor woman. When Alexei attempted to offer her a higher salary, she categorically refused to return and continue working with Tim. He had no choice but to thank her for her work and bid her farewell.

After that incident, Alexei started working part-time so he could spend more time with Tim. He often watched him secretly but didn't notice anything unusual. Over time, Chen's story began to seem less plausible to him, and he gradually began to forget about it.

But once, when Alexei entered Tim's room, he saw the little boy sitting at the table, his head bent over a sheet of paper, drawing something, while a stone pistachio nut flew rapidly in circles above him. Hearing his father, Tim turned his head sharply toward the entrance, and the pistachio immediately clattered onto the floor.

"I must have imagined it," was the first thought that came to Alexei's mind. However, no matter how hard he tried to convince himself of this, he couldn't. He kept catching himself thinking, "I definitely saw the pistachio flying over Tim's head." He was tormented by guesses about what the hell was going on and tried more than once to talk to his son about it. But all his attempts were in vain: the boy stubbornly remained silent in response to his questions, just as he had once done with the local police officer.

3.

Time passed. The ransacking of the apartment and the flying bell were long gone. Tim started going to the same school where Alexei worked.

During his studies, the boy never asked his father for help and completed all his assignments on his own. Many subjects came very easily to the young student, and he was one of the best in his class. His teachers often praised him.

The only thing that worried Alexei about Tim was his introversion. The boy hardly communicated with his peers and had no friends at all. Alexei felt his son drifting away from those around him and from himself.

Tim's transition age was particularly difficult. Due to the teenager's stubbornness, it became increasingly difficult to communicate with him. At the age of 13, he became simply unbearable and completely stopped listening to his father. His stubborn silence in response to any words greatly annoyed Alexei and sometimes drove him crazy.

Once, Tim angered Alexei so much that he couldn't control himself and slapped him on the back of the head. The young rebel looked at his father with furious eyes. Then he lowered his head, slowly filled his lungs with air, and, opening his mouth slightly, exhaled sharply. As he did so, he let out a very strange squeal. The slightly open front door behind Alexei was knocked off its hinges and frame as if by an explosive wave. Tim slipped past and ran out of the room.

For some time after that, Alexei stood rooted to the spot, not daring to move. After recovering a little, he sat down on a chair and tried to collect his thoughts. Now he was sure that the flying stone pistachio was not a figment of his imagination. He decided to have a serious talk with Tim when he returned home.

After spending the entire evening at home, Alexei did not wait for his son to return and fell asleep at the kitchen table. Tim did not show up until morning. His father was exhausted and in a bad mood, so he and his son had another argument.

This time, Tim unleashed his anger on the wooden bookcase standing next to Alexei. The bookcase shook, and a moment later it burst into a strange blue flame and burned down in a matter of seconds. Nothing remained of it, not even smoke. The huge bookcase simply disappeared.

However, the wave of hot air severely burned Alexei's back and neck. The hair on the back of his head was singed, and his jacket caught fire. His head was splitting with pain. The last thing he remembered was desperately trying to put out the flames on his sleeve.

4.

Alexei woke up in his bed and breathed a sigh of relief, thinking he had had a nightmare. But the pain from his burns convinced him otherwise. Tim was sitting next to his bed with his head bowed. Noticing that his father had woken up, he said:

"Why do you always scold me? You don't even try to understand how hard it is for me. I feel like an outcast everywhere: at school, on the street, at home. Wherever I am, people look at me like I'm a leper and talk behind my back. Everyone here is a stranger to me! You've become a stranger to me too!"

Alexei's face contorted with unbearable emotional pain at these words. He couldn't find anything to say, because it was true. Outwardly, Tim did not look Chinese. Despite his dark skin, his tall stature, European features, and long, straight nose set him apart from those around him. The teenager's words seemed to sober Alexei, forcing him to remove the veil from his eyes and see for the first time the nightmare his son was living in.

5.

Even his native Chinese language did not help Tim get rid of his outsider status, as people primarily focused on his appearance.

He didn't look Russian either. His dark eyes and thick, coarse black hair bore little resemblance to his Slavic roots. In addition, he had enormous ears of unusual shape and size.

Every summer, when he visited his grandparents in Russia with his father, Tim went through a real ordeal. His appearance was a source of ridicule from the local kids when he went out to play in the yard. His Russian, with its incorrect endings and stress patterns, as well as his complete lack of understanding of life in Russia, greatly hindered his ability to fit in with his peers.

Through the example of his own son, Alexei realized how difficult life can be for many children born to mixed marriages. Even in the 21st century, when the world had long been promoting democracy, equality, and brotherhood, many people still harbored misunderstanding and alienation toward those who differed in skin color and eye shape.

Chapter 2 Accident at school

1.

Tim's life became even more unbearable after the death of one of his classmates in his final year of high school. According to his friends, it happened right in the middle of a lesson. Xiao Li was standing in front of the class, reciting a passage from the textbook. Suddenly, he let out a wild scream, fell to the floor, and began convulsing until he fell silent.

The emergency doctors who arrived were unable to do anything. The boy was already dead by that time. The autopsy showed that Xiao Li died of a ruptured heart caused by severe pain shock.

The cause of this shock was revealed by an X-ray. Cracks in the form of straight transverse lines were visible on many bones, which looked as if they had been sawn through with a thin saw.

The thickness of the cracks did not exceed 0.1 mm. No one could explain how such thin transverse cracks could appear in the bones. The doctors performing the autopsy were even more puzzled by the absence of any damage to the skin, muscles, or blood vessels. It seemed as if the teenager's bones had been cut from the inside, as if with a laser.

That day, Alexei was teaching in another wing of the building as usual and did not yet know what had happened. During the lesson, the school principal, Mr. Wang, came in and asked him to step outside for a moment. In the hallway, he told Alexei about the incident in Tim's classroom. Finally, Mr. Wang added that before his death, Xiao Li had said something to his son. Promising the principal that he would talk to Tim, Alexei went to look for him during recess. However, Tim was no longer at school.

After work, Alexei immediately headed home, hoping to find Tim there, but their apartment was empty. Towards evening, the doorbell rang. Alexei immediately sensed that something was wrong. Standing on the doorstep were two men in plain clothes and a local police officer. They wanted to talk to Tim.

When Alexei asked, "What's going on?" one of them replied, "This is standard procedure. As part of the investigation, we need to question your son as the main witness."

"Investigation?" asked Alexei, completely confused.

"The causes of death of the teenager are very unusual. The autopsy revealed multiple bone injuries, indicating a violent death. But who could have inflicted them and how remains a mystery," explained the man in plain clothes. He also mentioned Miss Chen, noting that Tim was involved in both cases in one way or another.

2.

Without waiting for Tim, the investigators left, leaving a summons with the address where Tim was to appear the next day. It became clear to Alexei that his son was not a witness in this case, but a suspect.

Tim returned home well after midnight, completely unrecognizable. He was shaking all over. Without saying a word, he went to his room and locked himself in. Alexei slipped a police summons under the door and didn't bother him anymore.

The day after the police interrogation, Tim, as on the previous day, slipped silently into his room and did not leave it day or night. In the morning, Alexei decided to go in. The door was unlocked. His son was lying on the bed, curled up in a ball. He had a fever, and his body was shaking.

After a while, the fever subsided, and Tim began to slowly leave his room. Like a shadow, he moved very slowly and quietly to the kitchen and back. His father noticed that the young man had completely lost his appetite—as soon as he ate anything, he immediately began to vomit.

All of Alexei's attempts to talk to his son were interrupted by the latter's response: "Leave me alone! I don't want to see you!"

Once again receiving this answer, Alexei approached his son, grabbed him by the shoulders, and shook him. Then, without looking away, he stared intently into his eyes and asked the question again:

"Son, are you somehow involved in Xiao Li's death?" Alexei said quietly but clearly, without taking his eyes off the young man.

Tim remained silent, staring strangely at a single point in front of him.

"Did you do it?" Alexei asked again, barely audibly, and added:

"Don't be afraid, you can tell me."

In response, Tim nodded and began to sob.

Chapter 3 Tim's Disappearance

1.

After Xiao Li's funeral, classes resumed at school. Tim became an outcast, and even his teachers shunned him. Seeing how much he was suffering, Alexei advised his son to focus on his studies and not think about anything else. The boy listened to his father, began to study hard, and prepare for his final exams.

Alexei suffered no less than Tim, and the last few months before the summer holidays turned into pure torture for him. Unlike his son, he was not shunned, but the attitude of his colleagues and students towards him changed significantly. The former friendly and cheerful atmosphere was suddenly replaced by alienation, coldness, and formal communication.

In June, Tim received a very high score on the gaokao, a standardized test for university applicants in China. This allowed him to enroll in one of the most prestigious universities in the country, Peking University. Initially, he chose the archaeology department, having always dreamed of researching artifacts and remains of ancient civilizations. But at the last minute, Tim decided to switch to the medical department and began studying Chinese medicine, immersing himself completely in his studies.

Deciding to be closer to his son, Alexei also moved to Beijing, but they rarely saw each other. His son lived in a student dormitory on the university campus in the northwest of the city. Alexei rented a place on the other side of Beijing, near the Russian language school where he had started working as a teacher.

Years passed. Tim earned his master's degree in medicine and began writing his doctoral dissertation. During his studies, his appearance changed noticeably. He grew a beard, started wearing glasses and a Chinese-style business suit (a jacket with a small stand-up collar and wide, straight pants that did not restrict movement). His gait and movements became very smooth and slow. He spoke little and quietly. In his early twenties, he looked much older than his father, and no one believed that Alexei was his father.

Once, on the eve of the Chinese New Year, Alexei visited his student at the university. Almost no one was left in the dormitory — most of the students had gone home to celebrate the first day of spring with their families, as is traditional.

After greeting the receptionist and signing the visitor log, Alexei went up to the second floor of the small building where Tim lived. He walked down the hallway past several rooms and stopped in front of door number 18.

It was Tim's room. The door was unlocked, and Alexei entered after knocking several times. He found no one inside, and his face showed his confusion. He took out his cell phone and tried to call his son again, but, as in the last few days, the subscriber remained unavailable.

After sitting in the room for a while, Alexei went down to the receptionist to ask about his son. To his surprise, Grandma Zhen said that Tim rarely appeared in the dormitory, and she couldn't even remember when she had last seen him.

Alexei didn't know what could have happened to Tim. He was overcome with panic, but after calming down a little, he began to search for him. First, he went to the dean's office, but there he heard exactly the same answer as from the security guard. He was advised to contact the police and file a missing person report. He continued to search actively for Tim, but to no avail. His son seemed to have vanished into thin air.

2.

Alexei fell into despair. By the beginning of summer, he had completely lost heart and began to drink heavily. Seeing that Alexei was rapidly losing control of himself, one of his acquaintances contacted his elderly parents and informed them that their son was spiraling downward. They managed to get through to their son. In a long and heartfelt conversation, his loving parents persuaded him to return to Russia.

With great difficulty, Alexei made the decision to leave China, where he had spent his youth and adult years. Despite all the difficulties, he enjoyed his time in this country. The locals always treated him with respect and were ready to help him in times of need.

However, Tim's disappearance devastated Alexei. He felt miserable and lonely. First Nicole left him, and now his son was gone. He was completely broken and resented his fate.

3.

Still quite young, but already an old man at heart, Alexei returned to his homeland and settled in the Russian hinterland, where he was born. Mother Russia took the poor fellow back, without even noticing his absence. She shook him up with her harshness, ruthlessness, and heartfelt simplicity.

After spending so much time abroad, it wasn't easy for Alexei to live in his homeland at first. The contrast between Russia and China was huge. He shared his impressions and observations about this with his friends, and they responded by telling him he was living in the past.

Yes, Alexei's friends were right—he left China, but that country never left his heart. Memories of life in the Middle Kingdom often came back to him. He continued to read books and news in Chinese, leafing through Chinese Russian and Russian Chinese dictionaries.

He enjoyed listening to Chinese online radio. At the table, instead of a fork and spoon, he used wooden chopsticks, which seemed very unusual to his relatives.

However, over the years, the images from his past became less vivid. And more than 15 years after his return, he could hardly believe that he had ever been to China. The only reminders of his life abroad were the things he had brought back with him. Most of them were stored in the attic, and he would sometimes go up there to rummage through his past.

Once, while sorting through items brought back from China, Alexei came across a stack of notebooks tied together with string. They belonged to Tim. He remembered that a long time ago in Beijing, the guard at the student dormitory had given him his son's belongings, which had been left in his room after his disappearance.

Alexei became curious. He untied the rope and began to leaf through the notebooks one by one. Most of the entries were written in Chinese characters, and it was difficult for him to make out anything. Reading Chinese cursive is a science in itself and requires special skills. But one of the notebooks turned out to be written in Russian. This greatly surprised Alexei, because he was sure that Tim had never really learned to write in Russian.

It turned out to be a diary with personal notes...

Part 3 Tim's Diary

Ultrasonic control

My earliest childhood memory is of finding a stone bell in a sand pit and hearing it ring for the first time.

The bell rang when I squealed with joy. Apparently, my squeal accidentally reached such a high frequency that the bell's clapper vibrated and began to hit the walls. So the bell responded to my squeal with a barely audible ring.

The sound of the bell was very beautiful and unusual, reminiscent of birdsong trills—sometimes short, sometimes long. Its ringing could be heard every time I began to burst into cheerful laughter, or rather, squeal.

I really enjoyed playing with the bell. The louder I squealed, the stronger its response, which I found very amusing. I tirelessly imitated the bell, trying to reproduce its sounds. Gradually, the sound of my voice became more and more like its ringing, until it became exactly the same.

Over time, I learned to produce a sound with such a high amplitude that it could not be detected by the normal human ear. That's how I discovered my ability to produce ultrasonic at different frequencies.

Under the influence of ultrasonic, the shape of my ears has changed. They now resemble hollow orange halves and fit snugly against my head at a 23° angle. Thanks to this, I can perceive ultrasonic of any frequency. It's funny, but now I can hear radio stations without a radio receiver.

I constantly trained myself to control my ultrasonic voice and learned to use it like my hands. Now, with its help, I can easily lift and move objects of any size and weight. By adjusting the strength, speed, frequency, and direction of the sound wave with my mind, I am able to turn things into dust, cut them, and burn them to the ground, like a laser.

Like bats and dolphins, I can navigate in space using reflected sound signals. Thanks to ultrasonic beams, I see with my ears in the same way that a normal person sees with their eyes using light.

By emitting ultrasonic, I can clearly recognize the sizes and shapes of not only external objects, but also those hidden inside other objects. This allows me to see through walls, skin, flesh, and other materials. With ultrasonic, it's as if I'm pulling back curtains and seeing what's behind them.

The ultrasonic waves I direct can pass through human skin, muscles, and bones, destroying only a specific internal organ, a malignant tumor for example without damaging other tissues.

I learned to move through the air by sending powerful impulses to my feet and stepping on ultrasonic stairs right in the air. Over time, I became able to part the depths of the sea with my voice and pass through them as if through a corridor between walls of water.

To do all this, you need very strong lungs, and I have to train them constantly. I go jogging every day, and when I have time, I go swimming in the pool. Swimming underwater while holding my breath is especially helpful.

A transverse bamboo flute, which I don't remember who gave me as a child, also turned out to be very useful. This ancient Chinese wind instrument helps me control my breathing and practice different types of breathing: chest and abdominal. I always carry the flute with me and play it whenever I can.

Memory of the World Ocean

Water stores all sounds, recording their vibrations like a tape recorder records sound signals. With the help of ultrasonic, I can reproduce the sound of these vibrations.

I discovered this by accident when I directed a weak ultrasonic wave at a glass of water. To my surprise, I heard the phone ring and then my own voice. I remembered that I had received a call about an hour earlier and answered it.

I became curious to know whether water preserves the sounds of ancient times, as I have always been fascinated by history and archaeology. I decided to test this by listening to water from different lakes and rivers. However, I could only detect sounds that were no more than a century old.

Then I figured that the only place where sounds from the distant past could be stored was the ocean. Rivers flow into it, and they've been picking up everything that's been going on around them for thousands of years. Remembering that the city of Qingdao has access to the ocean via the Yellow Sea, I headed there.

I spent the entire summer at various beaches in my hometown. All day long, I listened to the sounds produced when the ultrasound I emitted passed through the waves.

What I heard resembled a radio broadcast with excerpts from old films: conversations, speeches, music and singing, the sound of merriment, battle cries, the moans of the wounded, crying, laughter, and much more from the lives of people of bygone eras.

At first, it was difficult for me to understand the sequence of events and who the people were whose voices I heard. But thanks to the ability to listen to the same part of the recording multiple times, I gradually figured it out and made some notes.

Now I know for sure that intelligent beings have lived on Earth for millions of years. One civilization has replaced another. The Earth, having witnessed many different cultures, has over time destroyed the traces of most of them.

Modern people do not even suspect that they are repeating the path of their predecessors. The civilizations that lived here before us had spiritual values and scientific achievements similar to ours. For example, like us, their theories about the origin of life on Earth boiled down to the accidental formation of organic substances from inorganic ones and the subsequent evolution of living beings, or were explained by a divine origin.

All civilizations that have ever existed on our planet have followed their own path of development. Most of them have strived for scientific and technological progress.

Technological advances have invariably led to population growth and the irrational use of natural resources. Highly developed technologies in the hands of selfish and mercenary political leaders have often been misused, leading to environmental disasters on Earth and mass extinctions of humans, even to the point of complete extinction.

There were also civilizations that destroyed themselves in internecine wars. Using powerful weapons against their enemies, they destroyed all living things, including themselves.

Only two civilizations have existed on our planet much longer than the others: the Potra civilization, one of the first and oldest on Earth, and the Kunlun Mountain civilization, the predecessor of the ancient civilizations we know.

Potra civilization

1.

About a billion years ago, the very first human civilization emerged on Earth. At first, these were wild tribes. Then states were formed. The strongest of them managed to conquer and unite all the others, becoming a huge and unique empire on the planet.

Over time, the inhabitants of this empire began to speak one language, use one currency, and obey a single set of laws. All cultural differences among the Earth's population completely disappeared.

The citizens of this state called themselves Potra. Possessing unique intelligence, they quickly passed through all stages of human development — from stone tools to high technology and space exploration. They were able to accumulate extensive knowledge about the micro- and macro-world, as well as achieve significant success in genetic engineering.

The Potra era was a period of the most advanced technology in world history. They created things that are difficult to imagine even for modern people. Science and technology allowed the Potras to achieve what no one else on our planet had ever been able to do.

For example, they replaced internal organs and body parts with artificial ones that looked and functioned just like the real thing. These organs, skin, and bones were made from super strong and lightweight material that never wore out.

The Potras could communicate by transmitting and receiving information directly to the brain using microchips embedded in their heads. Artificial eyes allowed them to see through objects. Prosthetic arms could transform into any tool or weapon. Prosthetic feet could be replaced with wheels or skis, and later were equipped with turbo engines for flight.

The lifespan of Potras has increased significantly thanks to the replacement of organs and body parts with artificial ones. The only thing that prevented them from living forever was the human brain. Although the electronic chips embedded in it improved human intellectual abilities, accelerating thinking and strengthening memory thousands of times over, brain cells still aged and died.

When all brain cells were completely replaced with artificial ones, a person turned into a cyborg, losing the ability to feel pain, fear, joy, and other emotions. Perception of reality became dulled, and along with the dying brain, the spirit of life faded away in a person.

2.

Gradually, material goods became more important to the Potras than spiritual values. They adopted a consumerist lifestyle, unaware that they had become parasites on Earth. In satisfying their needs, they caused enormous damage to nature and all living creatures on the planet.

Over time, Potra society began to divide into three classes. The first class consisted of people with healthy bodies. They did not yet need to replace their internal organs with artificial ones and could have children. These people occupied the top of the hierarchy and were considered the elite. They were called Elpa. They lived carefree, enjoying life to the fullest, knowing neither need nor hard work. The rest of society was engaged in providing material support and protection for the Elpas.

With age, as most of their organs were replaced with artificial ones, people from the elite class moved into the second class. People of this class were called Neopotra. They were completely submissive and served the Elpas, outnumbering them many times over.

When there were no real organs left in the body and the brain was replaced with an artificial one, Neopotras became cyborgs and moved on to the third class. Representatives of this most numerous class were called K-potra. They began and served as both Elpas and Neopotras. K-potras did not die. Their numbers were measured in trillions and continued to grow steadily.

Over the centuries, overpopulation and the complete depletion of the planet led to its total decline. Cataclysms began. Earthquakes and volcanic eruptions made life on Earth uninhabitable. Even the advanced technologies of the Potras could not protect them from such large-scale natural disasters.

At first, the Potras attempted to settle on other planets with solid surfaces orbiting the Sun. However, Mercury was even hotter and more scorching than it is now. The Potras' flying ships and technology quickly broke down, which made it impossible to create acceptable conditions for the elite to live in.

Venus encountered Potras with more powerful volcanoes than those that raged on Earth after the cataclysms began. Mars was also inhospitable in those distant times.

The planet Mars that is now considered most suitable for colonization was, millions of years ago, the site of giant sandstorms and strong winds that created conditions unsuitable for Elpas life.

As a result, the Potras decided to leave Earth and venture into outer space, hoping to reach the nearest exoplanet.

The Kunlun Mountain civilization

Many thousands of years ago, people with an extraordinary culture lived on Earth. They inhabited the Kunlun Mountains, where the Yellow River originates. These people learned everything from nature and sought to live in harmony with it. They revered nature as a deity, seeing in it the direct manifestation of the Creator.

These people were called Kunlun people. They spoke Cantonese, ate mainly plant-based foods, and went barefoot all year round. These people easily endured cold and heat. They rose at dawn and went to bed at sunset. Their days were spent in tireless work and study.

Over time, the Kunlun people learned to develop their mental, spiritual and physical abilities to superhuman levels. Such abilities could only be attained through constant probing at the limits of their knowledge. The Kunlun people called it "The Path to Heaven."

For those who accepted the challenge, the Path to Heaven was divided into three stages. The first was called the Stage of Humility and Prosperity. At this stage, the Kunlun followers of the Path sought spiritual purification and enlightenment. Injustice, disrespect, lies, theft, violence, and cruelty were not accepted in Kunlun society and were excluded for those who embarked on The Path to Heaven.

Food allowed was only plant-based. Meat, fish, eggs, and other animal products were forbidden. Gluttony and other forms of indulgence were also not allowed. Daily physical exercise and meditation helped strengthen the spirit and body of those who had embarked on the Path.

After completing the first stage, a person acquired spiritual purity and could proceed to the next stage — the stage of knowledge. In the second stage, the person gradually gave up water and food, as their body began to draw energy from the Earth and the Sun. This happened during meditation. The breathing and heartbeat of people immersed in trance slowed to imperceptibility. The breathless state during meditation increased: first it was hours, then days, and later months. By the end of the second stage, a person could remain in a breathless trance for more than a year.

Kunlun people who had passed the Stage of Knowledge were able to read other people's minds and see through any objects. They possessed hypnosis and telekinesis.

Such people were called the Lucent. They lived for an average of about 150 years and were mortal. Serving in monasteries, the Lucent were spiritual mentors for those who had just decided to embark on The Path to Heaven. They also often talked with those who did not want to embark on this Path and those who often strayed from it.

Some of the Lucent led nomadic lifestyles. They traveled the world and told different people about their teachings. The images of some of them were captured by ancient civilizations. Thus, the culture of Ancient India brought us the teachings of Buddha, and the culture of Ancient China brought us the teachings of Laozi. Both of them were the Lucent, and it is thanks to them that the modern world has learned about some of the ideas of the Kunlun teachings.

Not all the adherents to the Path to Heaven were able to complete the third stage — the stage of reunification. This stage consisted solely of meditation, which they conducted in complete solitude. Usually, those who had attained enlightenment would go high up into the mountains for this purpose. A person could remain in a trance for years until they completed the entire Path.

During prolonged trances, many of the Lucent died without achieving spiritual and physical perfection. The death of the body severed their physical connection with the higher mind of the Universe, and for them the Path to Heaven remained unfinished.

Those who were destined to walk the Path to the end could see the Creator with their own eyes. They called the Creator SO. SO appeared before them in human form. After meeting SO, they became superhuman. SO gifted them complete control over movement in space and time, showing them how to take on any form and transform one object into another. Having completed the entire Path, they continued to see the meaning of their existence in serving SO.

The Lucent completed the Path, or as they were called Fundi, lived beyond Earth, far away in space, in a special dimension where their ageless bodies immune to natural death continued to acquire enormous power. However, they could be destroyed by other beings, or simply by their own will.

The Fundi were SO's messengers and appeared to ordinary people in the form of spirits or agents in earthly guise. All ancient myths in one way or another testify to the existence of the Lucent and the Fundi.

Confession of grave sins

1.

I remember when I was in high school. The whole class teased me because of my ears. I felt like an outsider among my classmates and dreamed of finishing school as soon as possible, going to university, and becoming an archaeologist.

Once, at the end of the school year, Xiao Li was called to the blackboard during history class. The teacher asked him to discuss a paragraph that had been assigned as homework.

Xiao Li walked up to the blackboard and began talking about the Opium War. He described how foreign armies put pressure on the local population and how opium gradually spread throughout the country, leading to serious consequences for people and society.

Every time he mentioned foreigners, he would give me a challenging look. Then, at the end of his speech, he suddenly pointed his finger in my direction and said loudly:

"People like this once tried to take over our country, restricting the freedoms of our ancestors and spreading opium. But they failed. Our people persevered. We preserved our independence despite numerous attempts to enslave us."

This greatly embarrassed me. It was extremely unpleasant to hear such remarks directed at me. I glanced at the teacher, but she seemed so stunned by Xiao Li's behavior that she couldn't utter a word. A gloomy and oppressive atmosphere prevailed in the classroom.

I felt uncomfortable, but Xiao Li continued and continued, as if he had completely forgotten about propriety. Finally losing all sense of shame, he began to insult my parents and mock my appearance, humiliating me in front of everyone.

A rage flared up inside me that I could no longer contain. I passionately wished that Xiao Li would regret every word he had said about my mother and me, and that he would experience torments he had never known before.

2.

My mastery of ultrasonic voice was not that advanced at the time. I couldn't always control the strength and frequency of the waves accurately. Besides, at that moment, I wasn't thinking about the harm I could cause my classmate. My mind was clouded with hatred.

Taking a deep breath and slightly opening my mouth, I emitted several ultrasonic pulses toward my abuser. A few seconds later, Xiao Li collapsed to the floor as if he had been struck down. His body began to writhe in pain, and he groaned. A moment later, he began to shake violently. Soon his heart stopped, and he fell silent.

One of the students screamed, "鬼鬼！啊啊啊！ 4" and ran out of the classroom with a hysterical squeal. The rest sat frozen in deathly silence. As if petrified, with their eyes wide open, they stared at the lifeless body lying on the floor.

3.

After that incident at school, everyone started avoiding me. No one wanted to talk to me; they were afraid of me. When I walked down the hallway, entered the cafeteria or library, everyone fell silent. Some immediately ran away. I often heard people behind me saying, "There goes the devil incarnate."

---

4 guǐ guǐ! āāā! – Damn it, damn it! A-a-a-a! (transcription and translation from Chinese)

I always deeply regretted what happened to Xiao Li and blamed myself — after all, I took his life just because of a harsh word. Now I understand perfectly well that his speech in front of the class was just a manifestation of youthful exuberance — a crude but not malicious attempt to assert himself, albeit in such a disrespectful manner toward me.

4.

I continued to use ultrasonic even after Xiao Li's death. I don't know where this determination to fight evil came from. With ultrasonic vibrations, I punished everyone who took people's lives and caused others pain and suffering. The supersonic waves I emitted penetrated the criminals, striking them from within. My ultrasound also affected their consciousness, instilling in them a paralyzing fear of inevitable retribution.

I punished even those who were already behind bars. I didn't need to go into their cells or even approach the building itself. Instead, the ultrasound I had launched acted on my behalf. It became my eyes and hands, passing through walls and any obstacles.

At that time, I was convinced that there could be no forgiveness for their actions. In my view, each of them deserved retribution, and I believed that I was performing a true act of justice.

Now I deeply regret what I have done and pray to God every day for forgiveness. I once used to think that by taking the lives of villains, I was restoring justice. I did not realize that by responding to violence with violence, cruelty with cruelty, and murder with murder, I myself was becoming a villain.

Hearing tuned by a bell

The Holy Scriptures say, "In the beginning was the Word." I guess that "Word" means sound. I hear the movement of our planet and the Sun in space. Sound comes from everywhere, even from molecules and atoms, protons and electrons. Blood makes a sound as it moves through the blood vessels.

Our entire universe consists of sounds, or more precisely, energy pulses. These sounds are melodic and resemble classical music. It is incredibly beautiful, but humans are only able to hear a small part of this divine symphony.

At the age of seventeen, I realized that I could recognize people's feelings and thoughts by the specific sound vibrations emitted by their brains. This helps me identify criminals.

When a person thinks about committing a crime, their brain creates very chaotic high-frequency impulses. This may be because violence is contrary to human nature, and even thoughts of cruelty cause ultrasonic waves that stand out strongly against the general sound background.

I can pinpoint the source of these negative sounds, even if they come from other continents. Based on the strength and frequency of the sound waves, I can immediately tell whether a crime is being committed at that moment or is only being planned.

In turn, the heartbeat is also one of the strongest sounds in the universe, and it vibrates in unison with its rhythms. When I detect a disturbance in the harmony of the heart with the universe, I already know that something bad has happened somewhere. And if the heart of a person in trouble is still beating, I can find the place where a crime is being committed or a disaster has occurred, even more accurately than by the brain vibrations of the villains.

Realizing that I possess unique abilities, I decided to use them to defend justice throughout the world. I have always tried to go places where the most powerful negative brain vibrations or chaotic heartbeats originate. Moving through the air, I can quickly reach any point on the planet where evil and injustice are taking place.

I have repeatedly attempted to stop atrocities of all kinds, from mass murders and global catastrophes to military conflicts.

My constant travels around the world leave me no time to study. I rarely show up at the university and only come for exams. Water helps me pass my exams. I whisper the answers into a water bottle, as if it were a tape recorder. The teachers don't notice my "cheat sheet," which is in plain sight the whole time.

Meeting with my mother

The human heart has another distinctive feature — its beating rhythm. This unique heartbeat is similar in every person to the rhythms of their relatives' hearts and is almost identical to the sound of their parents' hearts.

Once, while in America, I heard my mother's heartbeat. This surprised me greatly, because my father had told me that she had died during my birth. I wanted to see her.

The place where my mother's heartbeat came from turned out to be a two-story mansion somewhere near San Francisco. From the similarity of the heartbeats that shared her living space, I realized that along with her, my grandparents were also in the house, as well as two teenagers—her children.

I rang the doorbell, and a few minutes later a very beautiful woman with Asian features opened the door. She smiled warmly and asked, "How can I help you?" My legs turned to jelly—standing before me was my mother, whom I had never seen before.

She looked no older than twenty-five, but the wrinkles at the corners of her eyes suggested she was much older. She was short, thin, and had a fashionable short haircut. She was wearing red pajamas. On the ring finger of her left hand, she wore a ring with a huge blue diamond, and in her ears, she wore small stud earrings with the same stones.

After I told her my name and mentioned my father Alexei, the smile immediately disappeared from her face, and a look of alarm flashed in her eyes. She stared at me intently, then said very rudely, "I don't know who you are, and I have no idea what you're talking about. You must have me confused with someone else." Closing the door, she added, "If you show up here again, I'll call the police."

Behind the door, she could be heard saying loudly to someone in Cantonese: "Some kind of bum! They've become completely insolent..."

After standing on the porch for a while, I wandered off. I was devastated, I began to wander aimlessly through the streets in the drizzling rain, playing sad melodies on my flute.

Holy beggar

A few hours later, I found myself on the outskirts of the city. The road I was walking along crossed a high-speed highway and passed under it like a small river under a bridge. The section of road under the highway was well protected from rain and heat and served as a shelter for homeless people who had pitched their makeshift tents there.

Several people were standing by the tents. They looked like either drug addicts or alcoholics. An elderly woman was sitting in a wheelchair next to them. Their dirty clothes gave off a strong stench. Another resident of this place was sweeping the sidewalk. It was clear from the faces of some of them that they were suffering from mental disorders.

A little way from the tents stood two plastic toilet cubicles and two rubbish bins: one was filled to the brim with glass bottles, and the other with ordinary rubbish. Near the bins were many shopping carts taken from the supermarket. On the other side of the road lay a pile of broken bicycles, and a guy was sitting nearby, repairing one of them.

As I was walking past the tents, I suddenly heard a woman's voice. It sounded special somehow — very soft and melodic. I turned my head and saw a girl talking to one of the homeless people. I stopped and watched her. Suddenly, she turned around and looked me straight in the eyes. Her gaze radiated some kind of extraordinary energy that penetrated deep inside me. That look immediately made me feel warm and calm.

She had Asian features: black almond-shaped eyes, dark straight long hair, an oval-shaped face, and a slender build. Just below the center of her forehead, right above her nose, she had a large mole that looked like a third eye or a colored bindi dot like Hindu women wear. She was wearing a T-shirt and worn jeans. Her feet were bare.

Later, I learned that she walks around the neighborhood, collects alms, and brings them to places like this tent camp to help the homeless. They said she could heal with her words: after meeting her, the insane would regain their sanity, the blind would begin to see, and the paralyzed would stand on their feet.

Some explained this by saying that she heals not the body, but the soul, and thanks to this, people find hope, their lives improve: bad luck is replaced by good luck, the unhappy find peace and joy, and the disappointed find meaning in life again.

I couldn't explain to myself how and why she had become homeless. No one knew who she was or where she came from. It was difficult to take her for a vagrant: she had a noble bearing and a gaze full of wisdom and calm. Her clothes were always clean, and she exuded a subtle, fragrant aroma.

Usually, I can accurately determine a person's gender, age, and health by their pulse. But her heartbeat suggested that she was over 12,000 years old. I couldn't believe it and decided that I was mistaken, because she looked no older than twenty.

The desire to start a new life

I increasingly blame myself for not using my abilities wisely—I studied to become a doctor, but instead I maimed and killed people, even if they were scum they didn't deserve to die. At the time, I didn't understand that by using ultrasonic in medicine to treat diseases, rather than to fight villains, I could have saved many more people and helped the world eradicate evil and injustice simply by healing people.

When I met that girl in San Francisco, I saw that compassion can work wonders, and that mercy can heal not only the soul, but also the body. Something inside me changed. I suddenly realized that violence cannot be eradicated with cruelty, and that my evil deeds do not make the world a better place.

I think about her all the time, and no matter how hard I try, I can't forget her. I think I've fallen in love with her. I don't see her as a beggar, but as a saint. The crazy idea of dropping everything and going to America just to be near her and follow her around won't leave me alone. I'm sure she'll feel the same way about me because I heard her heart start to beat faster every time she looked at me...

***

That was the last entry in Tim's diary. The mention of San Francisco gave Alexei at least some clue. It gave him hope that he would be able to find his son, and he decided to go to California.

Part 4 The Healer Shen Yun

Chapter 1

I was only able to fly to America a year after finding the diary. It took me just a few months to get a tourist visa, but I had to work hard and save almost everything I earned to earn enough money for the trip and unexpected expenses.

California greeted me with bright, scorching sun and friendly smiles. After settling into one of the local hotels, I began searching for the girl described in Tim's diary.

"I'll find her, and I'll find Tim too," I decided, and began searching for her everywhere homeless people and vagrants lived in San Francisco. It wasn't difficult to find homeless people in this metropolis. They could be found in many places, even in the city center, right at the entrances to expensive fashionable stores against the backdrop of skyscrapers.

There were many tent cities with destitute and disabled people, but I did not lose hope or determination. Every day I went around them one by one, asking the locals about a barefoot saint with a large mole on her forehead. Some said they knew her but had not seen her for a long time. Someone mentioned that lately she always came with some big-eared guy.

No sooner had I arrived and begun my search than a nationwide quarantine was declared due to the deadly Gofit virus. This virus was extremely dangerous and claimed the lives of millions of people around the world. It entered the body through the respiratory tract and attacked the lungs. Gradually, the infected person began to suffocate and died.

To stop the spread of the virus, transport links between countries were suspended. The work of institutions, enterprises, plants, and factories was suspended. Concerts, sporting events, and other mass events, both local and international, were canceled.

The high mortality rate from the Gofit virus kept everyone in fear. San Francisco, like other large cities, seemed to have died out. On the streets, where crowds of people used to walk, only occasionally could you meet a lone passerby. There were almost no cars on the roads, and most residents did not dare to step outside.

People stayed at home for weeks, as if in a bunker, daring to go out only to buy food when their supplies ran out. The shelves of grocery stores were emptied within hours of opening. Everything was sold out instantly.

Many simply went mad during their confinement in their own apartments. As survivors later admitted, the isolation was harder to bear than the virus itself.

Over time, people adapted to life in a world ruled by Gofit. Masks and hand sanitizer became essential items for everyone. It was not permitted to walk down the street or be in public places without a mask.

 Long lines at supermarkets, where only a few people were allowed in at a time, became a common sight. Waiting in line for hours just to get into a grocery store became the norm.

Chapter 2

1.

Once, while standing in one of these lines, I overheard a conversation between the people in front of me. They were Chinese immigrants. To pass the time while waiting in line, I pricked up my ears and listened to their conversation in Chinese:

"This damn virus affects both the elderly and the young. Those with weak immune systems or chronic diseases are dying. Many people have already died in my hometown in China. Hospitals are overflowing, and there aren't enough doctors."

"My relatives from China called me. They said that a healer saved our grandfather."

"What kind of healer?"

"They say he lives in a village near Shenzhen. People line up for miles to see him. He heals patients with severe pneumonia when it seems that nothing else can help..."

They continued talking for a long time, but I was no longer listening. The story about the folk healer intrigued me, and I took out my phone and started searching for information on the Internet. It turned out that there was a lot written about him on Chinese websites and chat rooms.

The healer was called "神韵 5". They wrote that he not only saved those infected with the virus but even cured cancer and AIDS. He treated people for free, without turning anyone away. Many

---

5 shényùn – Divine Sound (transcription and translation from Chinese)

considered him a saint. But there were also those who did not believe these stories, claiming that it was all fiction.

In one chat, someone wrote that Shen Yun does not look Chinese at all, even though he speaks Mandarin without an accent. Another participant added a comment about the healer's unusual appearance, mentioning his large ears, which resemble orange halves.

After reading this, I immediately guessed that it was about Tim. He didn't look Chinese, spoke Mandarin without an accent, and had huge ears — it was none other than him. I was very happy about this, because now I knew exactly where to find him.

2.

A few months later, scientists from different countries managed to create a vaccine for Gofit. The death rate began to decline, and soon the borders between countries reopened. Flights between America and China resumed, and I was able to fly directly from San Francisco to the Middle Kingdom.

Arriving in Shenzhen late in the evening, I spent the night in a small hotel near the airport, and in the morning, I went to the village of Honglong, where the so-called Shen Yun lived and practiced medicine. My modest budget did not allow me to take a taxi or rent a car, so I had to get there by public transport.

When I got off at my stop, I immediately saw a huge crowd of people near the road. People were slowly moving in a column along the road to the village of Honglong. There were cripples, old people, and young people in this line. Many had children in their arms. The seriously ill and those who were dying were carried on wheelchairs.

Joining the column, I moved with the others toward the village, which was still several kilometers away. After waiting for several hours, I had moved no more than a hundred meters from the place where I had gotten off the bus. Behind me was already a long line of people who had arrived later.

Towards evening, slowly moving behind those in front of me, I noticed a house in the distance with a line of people stretching toward it. It was Shen Yun's house. From time to time, the sound of flute music could be heard coming from there. As I got closer, I was finally able to see the healer himself.

He had long hair with gray streaks, braided into a plait that hung down to his waist. His stern, deeply wrinkled face was clean-shaven and deeply tanned. He was wearing a black tracksuit and white sneakers with black and blue stripes on the sides. I didn't recognize him as my son right away.

Tim received patients right on the porch of his house. He spoke very quickly and concisely. Each patient's treatment took him no more than 2–3 minutes. He opened his mouth slightly, emitting a barely audible squeak, similar to the squeak of a dolphin. After dismissing one patient, he immediately called the next.

When there were only a few people left in front of me in the queue, Tim suddenly looked at me without any surprise, as if he knew I would come. He looked into my eyes long and intently, then turned his gaze back to his patient and continued his work.

Finally, it was my turn, and we found ourselves face to face. I couldn't help myself and smiled broadly at him. Tim, without smiling, said coldly and quietly in Russian, "Come into the house." Then he turned to the people standing behind me in line and said, "I'm sorry, I'm not seeing anyone else today. Come back tomorrow." As soon as I entered, he followed me and closed the door. We hugged, and tears welled up in both our eyes.

Chapter 3

1.

Tim had changed dramatically. There was no trace left of the image I had kept in my memory for many years. His former arrogance and pomposity had also disappeared, as had his glasses. He behaved very simply and relaxed. All his movements were striking in their ease and calm rhythm. Only his eyes stood out sharply against the background of his peaceful appearance with a slight smile—in them, one could see great sadness.

"It's like this almost every day!" Tim suddenly said excitedly. "No sooner have you treated one patient than another arrives. It feels like I'm bailing water out of a sinking boat, but the water just keeps coming and coming."

"Well done, son. It's no wonder people call you a saint. But don't forget to rest. You heal others, but yourself…" Before I could finish, two little ones came running in from the next room, shouting, "Daddy, Daddy!" They ran up to Tim and hugged him from both sides, pressing themselves tightly against his legs. They were barely as tall as his waist, so they could only wrap their arms around his legs.

They were twins — a boy and a girl, no more than five or six years old. With dark hair, swarthy skin, and brown eyes, they looked very much like Tim. They had the same big ears as he did.

"Hey, kids, look who's come to visit us! It's your grandfather from Russia. I've told you a lot about him," Tim said to the children in Russian. They looked at me and were completely taken aback.

"Hello! Grandpa has come to visit you," I tried to start a conversation. But no matter how hard I tried, they remained silent, staring at me with their big eyes.

"They're shy," Tim said with the same smile, then added, "Okay, let's go have dinner," and led us all to the kitchen.

2.

After dinner, Tim took the kids to their room to put them to bed. I cleared the table and then started washing the dishes. When I finished, the house was so quiet that I could hear the cicadas chirping and the birds singing outside the windows.

Tim still hadn't returned, so I decided to look around the house. It was clear that the renovation had been completed recently: the floors, walls, and windows sparkled with newness and cleanliness. The kitchen and living room were furnished with expensive furniture and modern appliances.

In the hallway, there were stacks of five-liter bottles of drinking water on the floor. Next to them were boxes of fruit: bananas, apples, oranges, lemons, and kiwis. On the shelves of the kitchen cabinets were canned goods and glass containers with grains and nuts. The double-door refrigerator was stuffed with food and groceries.

The living room was dimly lit. A dark burgundy carved wooden shelf was attached to one of the walls at a height of about two meters. On it stood a small statue of Buddha, a bowl of fruit, and a vase with burning incense sticks. Several small electric lamps in the form of Chinese red lanterns were placed along the edges of the shelf, emitting a soft light. The room was cool and filled with the aroma of incense, like in a Buddhist temple.

In the opposite corner of the room, at the same height, hung another hanging shelf. On it stood an Orthodox icon of St. Nicholas the Wonderworker, and next to it lay a Bible. A small candlestick with three burning wax candles stood next to the icon. Seeing the various altars in the house, I suddenly remembered the phrase: "All religions teach about the same God, calling him by different names." Without realizing it, I became lost in thought.

While I was thinking about the unity of being, Tim quietly left the children's room. He replaced the candles in the candlestick of the Orthodox altar and lit them. Then he stood in front of the icon and began to pray. Noticing him, I decided not to disturb him and went out to the kitchen.

On the wall, next to the kitchen table, there is a cheerful painting depicting mountains and a river flowing down from them, over which a white cap of fog hangs. Chinese painting gave the kitchen a special atmosphere of mystery, awakening old memories in me.

Once upon a time, in the Middle Kingdom, I practiced calligraphy and visited museums displaying paintings by the great masters of old. All of their works extolled the immortality of nature in the form of mountains and pointed to the spiritual emptiness of people, which could only be filled by contemplating this nature.

There were two wooden stands by the windowsill, on which lay an ancient musical instrument – a guqin. Seven silk strings were stretched across its oblong wooden body, which was 120 cm long and 20 cm wide.

I know that playing it is very difficult: beautiful sounds are created when the fingers of the left hand press and vibrate the strings, while the right hand touches them on the other side, reminiscent of the technique of playing the guitar.

In ancient times, people used the guqin to calm their souls and suppress their base instincts. Its sound has been enjoyed for thousands of years.

Two small photographs of a young Chinese woman were stuck on the guqin. In one photo, the girl was sitting at the kitchen table laughing, holding chopsticks in her hand. There were many different dishes on the table in front of her. The photo was taken here, in this kitchen. In the other photo, the same girl was playing the guqin. From the large mole on her forehead, I guessed that it was En.

3.

After a while, Tim returned to the kitchen and offered me some tea, which I gladly accepted. He turned on the gas stove and placed a large metal teapot on it. When the water boiled, he rinsed the porcelain cups and a small teapot made of dark red Yixing clay with boiling water. Returning the kettle to the stove, he took a metal jar with a beautiful label and the Chinese characters "大红袍 [6]" from the cupboard. After pouring a few dark green tea balls into the teapot, Tim waited for the water in the large metal kettle to cool slightly, then poured it into the teapot and closed the lid.

"Yixing clay teapots have pores that allow the tea to 'breathe' while brewing. This gives the drink a special flavor," I recalled the words of a teacher who introduced our class to the tea ceremony many years ago in China.

After waiting no more than 20 seconds, Tim began pouring tea into cups, first into mine, then into his own. I knew that if he steeped the tea any longer, it would become too strong and bitter. Oolong, one of the most famous types of tea in China, is quite temperamental.

During tea, Tim talked a lot about his patients, their illnesses, and their treatment. He talked about how, after miraculous healings, many people brought money, gifts, and offered any kind of help. "Everything in the house and in the refrigerator, and even the house itself, are gifts from people in gratitude. I refuse and even forbid

---

[6] dàhóngpáo – *"Big Red Robe," a variety of Chinese tea grown in the Wuyi Mountains, Fujian Province* (transcription and translation from Chinese).

them to bring anything, but they bring it anyway," he said with a modest smile. Once again, I was more surprised not by what he was saying, but by the changes in him. Before, you couldn't get two words out of him, but now I couldn't get a word in edgewise as he continued to talk.

4.

"Is that their mother?" I asked Tim, pointing to the photos of En as he began to make tea for the second time. Tim glanced at me quickly, then looked at the photos. He smiled as he looked at the pictures. He just nodded in response to me.

An awkward silence ensued, which Tim broke after a while with a new story: "After we got married, I suggested that we leave America. I didn't like it there. I was constantly drawn back to China. En didn't want to move for a long time, but when Yan and Yana were born, I convinced her that living with children in China would be much cheaper and safer, and she agreed.

After we moved, I worked as a doctor, while En spent most of her time at home with the children. She became a wonderful mother. The little ones adored her and listened to her in everything. They loved playing with her and enjoyed listening to her fairy tales.

Once, I was putting the children to bed with her, and when she told one of her stories, it seemed to me that I had heard it somewhere before. The story was about ancient people who lived on Earth long before us. They lived in the mountains, honoring their customs and having a close connection with nature. But most importantly, these people knew how to become superhuman and gain immortality by passing through the three stages of the Great Path to Heaven.

"Kunlun people," I said.

"Yes," Tim continued, "and in some of her other tales, I heard the same thing that the ocean had told me. When I asked her where she got those stories, she said she had seen them in her dreams."

"Did she ever tell you anything about herself?"

"She did, but very little. Once she mentioned that she was raised by her grandparents and that she had never seen her parents. She only remembered some fragments from her past, that her grandfather called her En, and that she started wandering when her grandparents died."

"Where is she now?"

"She disappeared. It's as if she vanished into thin air. I looked for her everywhere, but it was all in vain."

"How long ago did that happen?"

"It's been over a year now."

Tim became gloomy and didn't say another word. He was lost in thought, completely forgetting my presence. I finished my tea and went to lie down on the sofa in the living room, leaving him alone.

After staying with Tim for almost a month, I returned to Russia. Tim promised to visit me with his children and celebrate New Year's Eve together. However, this was not to be. Insectoids appeared on our planet on December 24, 2046.

***

This concludes Alexei's eyewitness account. His future fate remains shrouded in mystery. But the story continues—in the following chapters, readers will learn about the latest events on Earth and the fates of his son, En, and other characters.

Part 5 En's Dreams

Introduction

When Alexei asked about En, Tim felt his emotional wound start to bleed again. No matter how hard he tried to heal his soul with daily work and caring for his children, the pain of losing his loved one did not subside. He sat in the kitchen until morning, thinking about En. The only thing he had left of her were memories, and he spent the whole night in them.

En loved to play the guqin in the evenings. Every time she picked up this musical instrument, he would quietly sit down next to her and listen. Strumming the strings and playing some beautiful Chinese melody, she would begin to recount something from her dreams, always starting her story with these words:

"You know, I remember almost nothing about my life. No matter how hard I try, only one image from my childhood comes to mind: early in the morning, when I was still very young, I was helping my grandfather plant young tree seedlings in the garden and listening attentively to his words:

"Humans, seemingly the most intelligent creatures on Earth, rarely managed to find harmony with Nature. They often violated its laws, and for this it punished the guilty, unleashing all its power upon them: cataclysms, droughts, and floods. When nature was angry, it spared no one, and all living things perished. After that, many millions of years had to pass before the planet could recover and life could begin again. And everything started all over again — grass and trees began to grow again, the simplest living creatures appeared, and then animals and humans. Cities and countries with different cultures, languages, and knowledge were formed again. That's how it is in this world—life on Earth appears and disappears. And so it goes on and on."

In my dreams, I see different people and know their names and their entire life stories. Everything appears so clearly before me, as if it were happening in real life. And every time I remember my dreams, it seems to me that I have already seen all of this somewhere in the past, or perhaps in another life."

Then she begins a new story, reminiscent of a fairy tale or legend about what happened on Earth a long time ago, about distant people and forgotten heroes.

En told Tim a lot about Earth's past that had not been recorded by the world's oceans. It was as if Nature itself or SO, for some reason, did not want them to be remembered.

The First Story Ergos

"Ergos was born during the Kunlun era. He was one of those who passed all three stages of the Path to Heaven and became a Fundus. He completed the Path very easily and quite quickly. Having begun to serve SO, he stood out among the other Fundi for his special kindness and love for people.

SO liked this very much and made Ergos his closest confidant. He came to trust him completely and rely on him as he would himself. Over time, SO revealed many secrets of the universe to this Fundus and endowed him with even greater power.

But Ergos soon became proud. He wanted everyone to know about his power. Without SO's knowledge, Ergos began to descend to Earth. Possessing unlimited power, he began to use his superpowers on Earth for his own selfish purposes.

Through deception and cunning, Ergos, behind the back of SO, created his own kingdom on Earth and became its ruler. But even this was not enough for him, and he wanted the Kunlun people and other nations to accept him as the true Heavenly King.

Ergos promised to grant superpowers to all Kunlun people, even those who did not want to embark on the Path to Heaven or complete the entire Path. To become a Fundus, they only had to bow down before him, renouncing the true and almighty Creator.

The Lucent did not approve of this. They said that developing superpowers in people who had not completed the entire Path would lead to a disruption of the balance and laws of Nature. But Ergos was able to tempt many, even among the Lucent. His words were so sweet, and the promised superpowers so great, that many succumbed to temptation.

To the Kunlun people who had already become Fundi before Ergos began ruling on Earth, he promised that their superpowers would not disappear, even if they violated the rules of the Path to Heaven.

As a result, many Kunlun people bowed down before Ergos. Among them were quite a few Fundi. All Kunlun people who followed him were called rejecters of SO (Ota). Ergos, meanwhile, came to be known as the Yellow Emperor Huangdi."

Story Two The Ota and Their Children

"All Ota had athletic builds and beautiful appearances. Male Ota had clean-shaven heads, faces, and bodies. Only female Ota wore long hair on their heads. The Ota were proud of their beautiful bodies and wanted ordinary mortals to see their perfection. Therefore, unlike the Fundi, their figures on Earth did not radiate a dazzling light of their own accord, and their naked bodies remained clearly visible to the naked eye.

They began to live in different countries, but most of them settled on a mountain in the center of the North Pole. In the place where the Arctic Ocean now lies under a thick layer of ice, there used to be land. On it stood Mount Meru, about 3 km high. The weather there was warm. Chestnuts, magnolias, and cypresses bloomed.

Living in the world of ordinary people, the Ota did not obey any laws and led a dissolute lifestyle. They spent all their free time in their castles, indulging in all kinds of pleasures and amusements. As Ergos had promised, their superpowers never disappeared.

The male and female Ota felt an irresistible mutual attraction. But any intimacy between them ended in tragedy: when their souls and bodies touched, a tremendous energy was released, destroying them. Their bodies burst into flames and disappeared in a blinding light. Such is the peculiarity of superhuman bodies. The only ones with whom the Ota could connect and reunite in love while remaining unharmed were ordinary people.

Esoks

Ordinary women, seduced by the Ota, bore their children, who were called Esoks. These children possessed the gift of clairvoyance, could see the past, predict the future, hypnotize, and read minds.

Ergos, learning of this, began to send such children to live and serve in temples erected in his honor. Growing up, the Esoks became priests of these temples.

The Esoks priests always wore white robes with hoods that hid their heads. They communicated only with the rulers of states and members of their families. The sacred knowledge about the world and the true god of the Esoks, SO, was kept in the strictest secrecy. Ordinary people were forbidden to address them or even be in the same room with them. Upon reaching old age, the Esoks priests died without leaving any offspring. They were replaced by young servants, and so it was repeated over and over again.

Esoks, born in different countries and on different continents, interpreted the belief in Ergos as the true Creator, based on the culture and traditions of the local people. His image and name, the architecture of the temples in his honor, as well as the tombs of rulers in different parts of the world differed from each other, but at the same time, it was always possible to find something in common between them.

By the command of Ergos, the Esoks hid the fact that ordinary people could acquire superpowers through self-knowledge and self-improvement. Everything supernatural was attributed exclusively to Ergos and other deities he had created. This was done so that people would believe in their weakness and helplessness, be easily controlled, and, most importantly, remain distant from the true Almighty.

For glorifying Ergos throughout the world, he took the Esoks under his wing. At birth, he began to give each of them a small stone bell in the shape of a pistachio.

"I saw one of those bells with you and was very surprised," said En, pausing briefly in her playing of the guqin and looking at Tim. Then she continued playing a quiet melody and said, "The bells were created to teach ordinary people to hear and control ultrasonic. The Esoks learned this easily thanks to the unique phonetics of the Cantonese language, which they knew from their fathers. The sound of this language is very similar in nature to ultrasonic. The ability to pronounce sounds in different tones helped the Esoks master the technique of producing ultrasonic.

From an early age, the Esoks wore bells on a gold thread around their necks and never took them off. While the baby's bone tissue and cartilage were soft and pliable, the child's ear, under the influence of ultrasonic, took on the necessary shape to perceive ultra-frequencies. The Esoks' ears became similar to orange halves."

After these words, she paused again and looked at Tim, then continued her story:

"When a child began to hear ultra-high-frequency sounds, he gradually learned how to use them. With the help of ultrasonic, children began to communicate with each other at a distance, as well as to call their fathers and Ergos when they were not around.

As they grew older, the Esoks perfected their mastery of ultrasonic waves. They used them in construction, moving huge stone blocks weighing hundreds of tons. The ultrasonic frequencies were used like a laser to cut and saw giant stones, as if a knife were cutting through butter. Ultrasonic allowed massive stone slabs to be polished so smoothly that the joints were flawless, and it was impossible to insert even a needle between them.

Three or four Esoks could build a temple, tomb, or other structure in just a couple of months. No ordinary mortal could understand how a few servants managed to create in such a short time what ordinary people could not build even in decades, employing hundreds of thousands of workers.

All this was possible because ultrasonic has enormous power and is capable of destroying any material. It can pass through objects of varying densities, reflect off them, and propagate in both a straight line and a spiral trajectory. Only the human mind is capable of controlling and using the power of ultrasonic as a tool or weapon.

The buildings of the Esoks have stood for many thousands of years and have survived to this day. The Egyptian pyramids, Stonehenge in England, Machu Picchu in Peru, Puma Punku in Bolivia, Teotihuacan in Mexico, as well as dolmens in Korea, the Caucasus, the Urals, and Europe—all are the work of the Esoks.

Atlanteans

The Ota women enchanted sailors who had been at sea for a long time. From a distance, many sailors thought that these treacherous beauties had huge fish tails instead of legs. Having become pregnant by sailors, the Ota did not want to have children and tried to avoid motherhood. However, their bodies were unique, and the life that had begun inside them could not be terminated in the womb. Because of this, the Ota had to carry the fruit of their wombs to term and give birth.

They could not bring themselves to take the life of their newborn children, so they secretly gave the babies to the aborigines who lived on the small southern islands near Antarctica.

Since all biological processes inside the superhuman women proceeded differently, the children they gave birth to developed and grew much faster than normal babies. They grew to be very tall, up to three and a half meters, and had powerful physiques. They did not have superpowers, but they were distinguished by their unheard-of physical strength and high intelligence. These giants are known in Earth's history as the Atlanteans.

One of the ancient Egyptian temples in the city of Sais contains records of how the Atlanteans formed their state. It was located on an island between Europe and Antarctica. Egyptian texts recorded how the Atlanteans made military campaigns to the coastal countries of the Eastern Mediterranean, Egypt, and Athens.

When Ergos learned about the Atlanteans, he appeared before them with gifts in exchange for worship. But the children of the island did not recognize any Gods and rejected his offer. Ergos was enraged. He flooded their huge island, which was located somewhere in the Atlantic Ocean. The surviving Atlanteans moved to the South Pole and took refuge in the mountains of Antarctica, but Ergos caught up with them there and staged a bloody massacre.

The Ota women, unable to bear the horrific sight of their children being slaughtered, begged Ergos for mercy. He spared the few surviving Atlanteans but forbade them from contacting the people who worshipped him.

After what happened, the Atlanteans began to lead a secretive and very cautious lifestyle. Living in seclusion on the shores of Antarctica, they achieved great success in science and technology. All UFOs and flying saucers sighted in our time are the result of the Atlanteans' activities."

After telling this story, En began to cry. She had a premonition that something terrible was waiting for them and that they would all perish. En could not see in her dreams that the Atlanteans would be among the first to defend Earth against the insectoids in 2046. But the numerical superiority of their enemies would lead to the complete destruction of the Atlanteans.

Story Three The Era of Ergos's Reign

"After the traitor to SO descended to Earth with the Ota, his thirst for power and greatness finally blinded him, and permissiveness clouded his heart. SO's favorite had changed. At his behest, the Ota committed acts of tyranny and evil, causing people to suffer and live in constant fear. Even those who obeyed his laws and world order did not know what might anger Ergos or his entourage, or upon whom they would unleash their wrath.

With the help of the Esoks, Ergos placed people he favored on the throne and helped them rule their states. By his command, the rulers waged endless wars, exploiting and oppressing their people.

Ergos indulged in every manifestation of evil, cruelty, and debauchery. It seemed as if he wanted to eradicate all the laws and world order created by SO. The villain forced Ota to seek out and destroy people who sought inner development and tried to spread the principles of goodness and justice.

He promised pharaohs and emperors that after death they would continue to rule in the afterlife over all those who had been subordinate to them in life. To this end, the Esoks built tombs that served as portals to the afterlife.

When the ruler's body was left in the tomb, his soul passed through a portal and ended up in the afterlife, where it found everything that the deceased ruler had possessed during his lifetime. The souls of all those who had been his slaves or servants also ended up there.

Many temples built by the Esoks were places where kings, pharaohs, and emperors could personally meet with Ergos and speak with him directly, without intermediaries. When meeting with rulers, Ergos changed his appearance, becoming the way these people depicted and imagined him.

But among the Kunlun people, there were still many who refused to bow down to Ergos. They continued to honor Nature and SO, obeying their laws. For this, most of them were killed by the Ota. Those Kunlun people who miraculously survived hid wherever they could find refuge and at least some shelter."

Story Four Rokhan's Disobedience

"The Esoks understood perfectly well that Ergos was a liar. They guessed that thanks to his cunning and spells, SO did not know what was happening on Earth. They realized how great and powerful Nature was, that even Ergos and Ota, with their superpowers, were unable to subdue it.

Esoks was alien to the injustice in the society of the people who worshipped Ergos. They were saddened by immoral foundations, selfish and mercantile principles, and the loss of human kindness, honesty, and love for one's neighbor among people. They sincerely mourned those who did not follow Ergos, did not recognize his authority, and perished.

Without Ergos and Ota knowing, the Esoks started helping regular folks. They painted pictures and wrote stories about the rulers' deeds on the walls of temples and tombs, and they slipped in some math, chemistry, and astronomy stuff too. The Esoks tried to get the ruling elite to see reason using hypnosis. The Esoks telepathically transmitted knowledge of medicine, navigation, agriculture, and crafts to kind-hearted people who sought to help their people escape suffering.

They did not dare to openly oppose Ergos' will. But one day, on the Yucatan Peninsula in Central America, one of the Esoks named Rokhan persuaded his comrades to disobey. This happened at the top of one of the pyramids during a mass sacrifice in honor of Ergos.

As usual during the summer solstice, a bloody ritual of cutting out the hearts of living people was performed in all the temples of Ergos across the planet. Starting in the east, at exactly noon across the planet, the voices of the doomed victims rang out one after another in every temple. In unison with them, the Esoks used ultrasonic to praise Ergos, creating a powerful stream of negative energy. This stream spread sequentially from east to west while the Sun was at its zenith.

Ergos took great pleasure in absorbing such energy. He fell into ecstasy and remained in a state of bliss for a long time. However, this time, while in his jade castle in the Kunlun Mountains, he felt the flow of negative energy dry up earlier than usual, leaving him unsatisfied.

Hovering motionless in the lotus position one meter above the floor of the spacious hall of his monastery, Ergos opened his eyes and listened. Then he rapidly ascended high into the sky and, remaining in the same position, slowly flew westward.

Carefully examining his temples and pyramids on earth, he noticed that on one of the pyramids the victims had not been killed. They were all kneeling together with the Esoks. Their eyes were fixed on the sky. Raising their hands before them, they prayed, "O Great One, save us from the evil spirit and the demon in the flesh. Forgive us for our sins!

Ergos immediately figured out their plan to call upon SO, and rage took hold of him. He fell like a stone onto the top of the pyramid, right into the crowd, crushing several people. Under his feet, their bodies turned into shapeless bloody patties. Then he began to rip out the hearts of those who were praying and devour them. As he did so, the hearts of his victims still trembled in his hand, as if unwilling to die.

Covered in blood, Ergos began looking around for the Esoks. Spotting one of them, the demon leaped into the air and darted toward his victim. Flying toward him, he grabbed him by the throat with one hand. Lifting his victim and pulling him close, Ergos roared in an inhuman voice. The unfortunate Esok, kicking his legs in the air, turned gray with fear. The demon laughed and croaked, "You dared to doubt me?"

At that moment, Rokhan, standing behind them, let out a shriek and sent a supersonic wave into Ergos' back. The powerful sonic blast staggered the demon. Without letting go of the gray-haired Esok, the demon turned and saw Rokhan standing at full height.

"So it was you who started all this," hissed Ergos, and in an instant he was right in front of the daredevil. Grabbing Rokhan by the throat with his free hand and lifting him off the ground, just as he had done with the first Esok, Ergos whistled with an ultrasonic sound that began to squeeze the heads of his victims. Both Esoks groaned in pain. Blood flowed from their noses, then from their ears, and later from their eyes. Ergos continued to emit ultrasonic waves. Rokhan screamed in unbearable pain. His scream turned into a supersonic sound. In a semi-conscious state, the sufferer uttered in Cantonese: "Heavenly Father, save me..."

Ergos laughed haughtily. But suddenly, a very calm and soft voice in the same language sounded above him: "Stop, brother." The echo of this phrase sounded several more times. The voice sounded so contrasting against the backdrop of the unfolding horror that the villain involuntarily looked up."

Story Five The Battle of Fundi with Ota

"Lifting his head, Ergos saw three Fundi hovering in the sky. As he looked at them, his eyes turned yellow. He lowered his head for a moment, as if lost in thought. But then he looked at them again and fired a powerful yellow laser beam from his eyes. The three Fundi immediately disappeared, dodging the laser.

Ergos did not reach Fundi but immediately began slaughtering everyone at the top of the pyramid. He fired laser beams, incinerating those he hit. At the same time, he still did not let go of the half-dead Rokhan and the second Esok.

Suddenly, the three Fundi appeared in the sky again. Positioned on either side of the raging demon, they simultaneously fired three powerful ultrasonic waves at him. The first struck him in the head, and the yellow color in his eyes immediately disappeared. The second struck his hands, forcing him to unclench them and release Esoks. The third knocked him off his feet, but as he fell, he managed to regroup and launch a counterattack.

A fight broke out. Several Ota who were nearby immediately came to Ergos' aid. Very soon, all three Fundi were killed. Enraged, Ergos began tearing their dead bodies to pieces and scattering them in all directions, while the Otas finished off the remaining Esoks and ordinary people.

Suddenly, other Fundi began to descend to Earth. They too had heard Rokhan's plea, but decided to descend to Earth without SO's command only after the murder of the three Fundi. The newly arrived Fundi first tried to talk to the murderers and stop them peacefully, but they responded with an attack. A battle began, gradually drawing in more and more participants from both sides.

The Earth trembled from the superhumans' combat actions, for the destructive power of their superpowers was immense. Once again, our planet was enveloped in horror and terror.

The battle between Fundi and Ota reminds me of the legends of the battle of the gods, recorded by ancient peoples. Much of what I saw in my dream is reflected in the epics of Ancient India: how the gods controlled the elements, emitted lasers, caused huge whirlwinds, and threw powerful explosive pulses, how the Earth burned, and rocks were charred. Incidentally, I recently found out that in the ancient city of Mohenjo-Daro, you can still find melted stones that were exposed to very high temperatures as a result of those battles.

The Fundi could use their superpowers in the material world for a limited time. They needed to rest and recharge their strength, otherwise their superpowers began to weaken, which was explained by the law of conservation of balance in the material world. Only after resting in the incorporeal space were the Fundi' superpowers restored, and they could return to the earthly world to continue the battle.

In that battle, it often happened that the Fundi' superpowers disappeared before they had time to return to the otherworld. Continuing to fight in the bodies of ordinary humans, they were seriously wounded or killed.

The superpowers of the Ota did not disappear. Moreover, they fought using various tricks and dirty tricks. They used ordinary people as human shields and killed women and children, using them as bait. The Fundi sacrificed their lives to save the weak and innocent, but often failed, dying or being captured, where they died from the Ota's brutal torture.

The battle lasted several days and nights. All this time, superhumans on both sides fiercely exterminated each other.

But gradually the ranks of the Fundi began to thin, and they begged SO for help."

Story Six The Wrath of SO

"SO heard the pleas and moans coming from Earth. At first, he thought he was imagining it. But when he listened closely, he was horrified. It was the dying cries of his loyal Fundi. Along with them came the death throes of ordinary people.

In an instant, SO appeared on Earth. As soon as he appeared, all the surviving Fundi disappeared. Noticing the disappearance of their enemies, the Ota rushed to search for them, but suddenly saw the silhouette of a man. The blue light emanating from him was so bright that even the Ota, with their superpowers, turned away and covered their eyes with their hands, and soon fell down and pressed their faces to the ground, hiding their eyes from the blinding light.

Only Ergos, breathing heavily after such a long and exhausting battle, looked directly at the silhouette. He knew who it was and did not run away or hide. SO, hovering without touching the ground, approached him. They hung in the air opposite each other at a distance of no more than an arm's length, at a height of about a meter. Their silent duel of eyes lasted quite a long time.

Both were of equal height and athletic build. Both emitted a blinding bright light, but unlike the SO, Ergos's light was yellow. Both had long hair and beards: Ergos' hair hung down freely, while SO's was gathered in a bun at the back of his head, and his beard was longer and thicker.

The Lord waited for his favorite to repent, but Ergos did not repent. He looked proudly and smugly at SO. SO thoughtfully lowered his head and remained motionless for a long time.

After a while, Ergos began to rise slowly. This was not happening of his own volition. Although he remained conscious, he was paralyzed and could not even move. Some invisible force was lifting him up very gently and slowly.

He couldn't breathe. Once he reached the upper layers of the atmosphere, he felt cold, and when he reached outer space, his body began to freeze. After 6–7 minutes of flight, the ice on him began to melt, and soon Ergos felt intense heat, which grew stronger with every passing second.

An invisible force continued to carry him, and he could not resist it. Soon Ergos saw that he was being carried straight toward the Sun. A thought flashed through his mind: "So this is the fate you have prepared for me," and he laughed loudly.

When Ergos was brought almost to the very center of the star, the invisible force that had bound him ceased to act. Control of his body returned to him. With great difficulty, he flew a short distance away from the sun's core, but the force of gravity was very strong and pulled him back. He had to use all his strength and power to overcome it.

The unbearable heat prevented him from concentrating. He didn't have the strength to disappear and move to another place. He couldn't do anything to escape the scorching heat. All his strength and consciousness were focused on fighting the high temperature and gravity of the Sun. His entire being was trying to survive in the 6,000-degree heat that could burn him in an instant.

After just a few minutes in the fiery furnace, his hair burned away, and terrible burns began to appear on his head and body. Ergos began to burn alive.

SO continued to stand with his head bowed all this time. Some of the Ota began to beg for forgiveness, and the Great One spared them. The rest shared the fate of Ergos.

After that, the silhouette of SO disappeared. As soon as this happened, the Earth's axis of rotation began to swing from side to side with great amplitude, like a spinning top. The sudden changes in the tilt of the axis caused the tectonic plates to shift. Earthquakes began, volcanoes erupted, and the water in the oceans shifted.

Inertial forces brought giant tsunamis crashing onto land. This led to enormous destruction. Most of the temples and tombs of Ergos were destroyed. Entire cities were buried under water, ice, and volcanic lava. Perhaps they are still there, keeping the secret of the terrible sin of the Kunlun people who renounced the true God.

The Earth's axis gradually stopped wobbling, but it remained tilted at an angle of 23.5° to the plane of the Earth's orbit around the Sun. The geography of our planet underwent changes. Many areas of land ended up at the bottom of the ocean, while places previously hidden by the sea became habitable. It was at this time that the great migration of people began.

Now the sun's rays merely skim the surface of the poles, bringing no warmth. The air temperature at the North and South Poles has dropped sharply, and where the Ota once lived on one side and the Atlanteans on the other, ice and snow now reign supreme."

Part 6 The Potras' Queen

Chapter 1 Life of the Potras in Outer Space

The Potras flew to the nearest exoplanet called Proxima Centauri B, hoping to find conditions there as suitable for life as on Earth. But their hopes were not fulfilled. The data about this planet, obtained on Earth using telescopes, was not confirmed. Flying to the next exoplanet, they did not find what they were looking for there either.

During their cosmic wanderings, the Potras continued to work on finding new sources of energy. After several hundred years of living in outer space, they discovered Ra energy. This energy was much more powerful than nuclear energy. Using the technologies they had developed, the Potras were able to extract this energy from stars and store it in special tanker ships. The star from which all Ra energy was extracted was dying, and the Potras flew on to the next one.

Not all stars were suitable for extracting this energy. When working with supergiant stars, explosions often occurred, causing enormous damage to equipment and personnel. As a result, Ra energy was only extracted from dwarf stars, which made the extraction process more controllable. The presence of planets with solid surfaces orbiting small stars helped reduce costs and speed up the work.

The Potras did not find any planets with conditions similar to those on Earth in any of the galaxies they visited. Therefore, their long stay outside Earth's conditions had a strong impact on the Elpas — they began to physically and mentally deteriorate. To save their elite, the Potras began to create artificial planets the size of Earth and place them in orbit around any dwarf star with a diameter similar to that of the Sun. Thanks to precise calculations, the temperature, water circulation, atmospheric pressure, landscapes, and many other factors on the satellite planets did not differ from those on Earth. This helped the Elpas survive and continue their lineage.

When the Potras left Earth, their population reached one hundred billion people. After discovering Ra energy and beginning to create artificial planets, the number of Potras continued to increase exponentially.

There were so many Potras that they gradually colonized thousands of galaxies, where their artificial planets revolved around almost every dwarf star. Galaxies and artificial planets were given names, like countries and cities, and star maps were created of the territories where the Elpas lived. They visited each other and traveled. Sometimes their tourist trips lasted several decades.

Chapter 2 The Coup d'État

Among the Neopotras there was a woman named Jedzala. She could not come to terms with the idea that her brain would soon die and she would lose the ability to feel and enjoy life.

It is known that, while still on Earth, many Neopotras tried in every way to prevent aging and death of the brain. They developed technologies for growing human organs. However, artificially grown brains were inferior to living ones in many ways. Their experiments with cloning and mutations are well remembered on planet Earth, because dinosaurs were born in the laboratories of the Neopotras. These giant reptiles died out only at the end of the Potra era due to cataclysms caused by this civilization.

When Jedzala saw how the elite began to revive and live even better than they once had on Earth, envy arose within her. Soon she was consumed by hatred for the Elpas, and she began to incite other Neopotras to stage a coup d'état.

Together, they began organizing terrorist attacks on artificial planets. The staged powerful explosions looked like accidents caused by technical malfunctions. As a result, many artificial planets, along with the Elpas, were destroyed.

Over time, Jedzala managed to take a leading position in Potra society and almost completely subjugate the Neopotras and K-potras.

The surviving Elpas attempted to restore the previous order. They persuaded the Neopotras to return to their side, and ordered the K-potras not to obey Jedzala, accusing her of crimes and declaring her a criminal.

A war broke out between Elpas' supporters and Jedzala's supporters. But there were more supporters of the new regime among the Neopotras, and after several decades, all adherents of the old order were destroyed.

Having suppressed the last pockets of resistance, Jedzala proclaimed herself Queen of all Potras. Her first decision was to carry out a bloody purge of the entire deposed elite. She showed such cruelty toward the Elpas that even her loyal Neopotra comrades were shocked.

Over time, Jedzala's natural brain became obsolete and was replaced by artificial intelligence. After that, she turned into a maniac, thirsty for endless energy enrichment and ready to destroy anyone who stood in her way. Under her influence, the Neopotras and K-potras also became obsessed with energy enrichment. Thus, the sole purpose of the Potras gradually became the acquisition of unlimited resources from any energy source.

With the advancement of technology, the Potras were able to extract Ra energy even from supergiant stars. They became like cosmic locusts. Flying from one star to another, they destroyed entire galaxies. The Potras continued to do this despite the fact that they did not need such enormous reserves of energy.

Many of the stars we see in the night sky were destroyed by the Potras long ago, but their light from the distant past is only now reaching our planet.

Part 7 Ergos's Daughter

Chapter 1 Refusing to be Fundus

1.

En had never seen her parents. Her mother died in childbirth, and nothing was known about her father. She was raised by her grandparents, her mother's parents. They were Kunlun people who miraculously survived the war between the Ota and Fundi and managed to survive the cataclysms and floods that befell the Earth after those battles.

The girl was very bright and quick-witted, and the elderly couple marveled at her precocious wisdom. They talked to their granddaughter as if she were an adult and even listened to her in many ways. Her grandfather was almost blind, and when her grandmother fell ill and could not get out of bed, their seven-year-old granddaughter became their only source of support and comfort.

From her grandfather, En learned about the once-great civilization of the Kunlun people. He told her about the history of these people, their laws and way of life, and how Ergos betrayed SO and began to rule on Earth. From him, she also heard about the Ota, the Esoks, and the Atlanteans.

Grandfather never spoke about the girl's mother. However, grandmother often remembered her daughter and frequently told En, "You look just like your mother! You are as beautiful as she was." From her grandmother's stories, En learned that her mother had been married off early to a Kunlun man who later joined the Ergos. After the wedding, he took her away and forbade her to see her parents. But one day, on the eve of the end of the war with the Ota, her mother returned to her family home. She was pregnant and due to give birth soon. The unfortunate woman died right in front of her parents, who were helping her give birth. The grief of losing their daughter severely undermined their health, and their granddaughter became their only consolation.

After both her grandmother and grandfather passed away, En decided to embark on the Path to Heaven. Her grandfather had told her about the path of self-development and enlightenment. Having made this decision, she began to live the life of a hermit somewhere high in the Kunlun Mountains. After several years of seclusion and asceticism, she became completely immersed in meditation.

During her journey along the Path, En was amazed at how quickly she was able to complete the first two stages, knowing full well that it usually takes at least 60 years. "Each stage prepares a person physically and psychologically for the next. To reach the second, and even more so the third stage, you need years of daily training," En often recalled her grandfather's words. At that time, she could not yet know whose blood flowed in her veins.

The young girl felt something special within herself that helped her pass all the tests with such ease. By the time she completed the third stage of the Path and became the Fundus, she was not yet twenty years old.

2.

When En became the Fundus, all the secrets of the world were revealed to her. She saw the process of the creation of the universe, the history of Earth over millions of years, and much more that is hidden from ordinary people.

Upon learning that she was the devil's child, En was overcome with horror. The unfortunate girl lost her peace of mind. She was weighed down by guilt over her father's deeds, and she began to feel her life energy gradually fading away. Broken and exhausted, she fell into a trance and remained in a state of non-existence for a long time.

With great difficulty, En managed to overcome herself and restore her mental balance. She saw her destiny in atoning for her father's guilt by taking on the suffering of the homeless, the crippled, and the orphans and sharing their fate. So she decided to return to the world of humans.

After descending to Earth, En suppressed all her superpowers. The only thing she couldn't get rid of was her clairvoyance. In her dreams and in reality, she was constantly haunted by visions of events from the past and sometimes from the foggy future.

En began to live among the abandoned, rejected, and unwanted. She voluntarily became one of those whom people tried not to notice and whom most of those who were fortunate in life considered outcasts of society. Having become an ordinary person again, she spent many years wandering and vagrancy, experiencing much suffering and grief.

Having accepted this life, En saw how much evil there was in the modern world of humans and realized that they themselves were the cause of it. She was struck by the fact that they did not even realize how fragile their world was, constantly balancing on the edge between good and evil.

Chapter 2 Return to Heaven

When En first saw Tim, she immediately knew that this man was her soulmate. Her heart responded to his courtship. Soon they started a family, and years later, their home was filled with the sound of children's laughter.

En was happy in her marriage. But after several years of happy married life, she began to be tormented by the same vision. In it, a black cloud slowly moved through space, engulfing stars and planets in its path. Gradually, it approached Earth, and darkness enveloped everything.

Over time, anxiety and fear completely overwhelmed her. She became increasingly worried about the future. A heavy foreboding about the possible loss of her husband and children gave her no peace.

En found solace only in prayer. Kneeling before images of saints of various faiths, she felt a little calmer. Gradually, she began to meditate more often and for longer periods of time. Once, while in a trance, she imagined how the Kunlun people practiced the Path to Heaven. She realized that only by becoming Fundus again would she have any chance of protecting her loved ones.

For a long time, she hesitated and couldn't decide whether to walk the entire Path to regain her superpowers. However, overcoming her doubts and fears, she stepped onto the Path to Heaven for the second time in her life.

Without explaining or saying anything to anyone, En left home and went to live in the mountains. In complete solitude, she began the Path, and thanks to her genes, she completed it in just a few years. Having passed all three stages, En reached the level of Fundi and returned to Heaven to once again serve SO faithfully, devoting herself completely to His Will.

Deep down, En held onto the hope that her superpowers would help change fate and save her family—even against the law of non-interference in earthly affairs, without the SO's command.

Chapter 3 A great loss

Several years had passed since En became Fundus again and returned to another dimension. Being in a special zone of outer space, she carried out SO's commands and could not know what was happening on Earth. Busy with heavenly matters, she was completely detached from reality and often remained in a trance.

One day during meditation, En suddenly heard Tim's desperate cry coming from Earth. Coming out of her trance, she saw Yan and Yana surrounded by Potras, while Tim was struggling with his last ounce of strength to break through the crowd of insectoids and try to save the twins.

Without hesitation, En rushed to the scene. As she picked up speed, her body transformed into a long purple laser beam about half a meter in diameter. The beam flew down to Earth, burning through hordes of ships and black warriors in its path.

But while En descended to Earth with a bright and powerful beam, the Potras managed to strike the children with volleys of fire. When she reached the spot, it was already too late — before her lay two little lifeless bodies, blackened by fire.

Earlier that day, Tim, returning to the shelter where Yan and Yana were staying, stumbled upon a group of Potras. He immediately engaged in combat and attempted to lure the enemies away from the children's hiding place.

The children remembered Tim's strict order not to leave the shelter under any circumstances. But when they heard the noise of battle and their father's cries from his wounds, the little ones couldn't stand it and ran out of their hiding place.

A multitude of black monsters immediately surrounded the children from all sides. Both children screamed loudly at the sight of these terrifying creatures. The two supersonic waves formed by their screams merged into one and struck the monsters closest to them. Knocked to the ground, the insectoids immediately got up and opened fire on the children.

Tim heard his twins screaming and tried to break through to them. He began to bring down enemies left and right, but he was unable to get through the crowd of angry black warriors. The shoulder wound he had received at the beginning of the battle prevented him from moving well and dodging shots. Very soon, he felt that he was almost completely exhausted. Meanwhile, the number of Potras was growing with every passing second.

Realizing that he would not be able to reach the children in time, Tim desperately shouted in ultrasonic tones, "Lord, save us!" Then, after a brief pause, he rushed at his enemies, shouting with all his might, "Please, help!" But, unable to dodge one of the laser shots, Tim was struck down instantly. In that battle, both he and the twins died a martyr's death.

Chapter 4 Entering the Warpath

What En feared most had happened—she had lost her entire family. At first, she screamed hysterically, and her ultrasonic screams swept away the Potras approaching her like a hurricane but then tears began to flow down her cheeks. Everything around her became blurry and distant, and her consciousness became clouded. Her will to live and fight left her, and she prepared to share the fate of her loved ones.

When En bent over the bodies of the children and began to mourn them, the Potras gathered around her again. Realizing that En was no longer going to attack, they decided to take her prisoner.

But as soon as the Potras approached her closely, several silver laser beams, each half a meter thick, suddenly rained down on the black soldiers from above. With each passing second, more and more beams fell from the sky onto the insectoids, and soon it seemed as if a laser rain had begun.

In each beam, a human silhouette could be seen. These were the Fundi who, hearing Tim's plea and then seeing what was happening on Earth, decided to stand up for the surviving humans.

Fundi entered the battle, appearing as if from nowhere and striking the enemy with a laser beam straight from oblivion, just as En had done. They all knew that they were violating the law of non-interference in worldly affairs without SO's command, but their love and compassion for people proved stronger than strict rules and prohibitions.

Seeing the laser rain, En's spirits lifted. She slowly wiped away her tears and, summoning all her willpower, joined the battle. Thus, En embarked on the path of war and eventually became the leader of Fundi. The war between Fundi and Potras began.

Part 8 The Feat of the Kunlun People

Chapter 1 Inside the Sun

During his very long stay in the Sun, Ergos' body and face were covered with ugly burns. Due to the high temperature, his skin peeled off in places, exposing muscles and tendons, and in some places the flesh completely melted away, exposing the bones. His appearance changed beyond recognition.

Staying alive and not burning alive required tremendous effort from Ergos. When he weakened and lost consciousness for a moment, he was immediately drawn into the very heart of the core. The heat relentlessly crept up on him and inflicted severe injuries. The pain forced him to wake up and move away from the sun's center as far as his strength would allow.

Over time, Ergos got used to the sharp pain and learned to go into a trance. During meditation, he had visions. Usually, they were of people killed by him or his band of renegades. He often saw ruined countries and destroyed cities that refused to recognize him as their god. He heard moans and cries. In his visions, he repeatedly witnessed people dying a martyr's death. But most often in his dreams he saw Rokhan, and his voice rang in his ears again and again, begging Heaven for help.

Trapped in the Sun's inferno, Ergos lived in torment for thousands of years. He lost track of time and had no idea how long he had been imprisoned. The prisoner of the fiery sphere could neither hear nor see what was happening outside.

Ergos was unaware that thousands of Ota were suffering alongside him, who had not repented before SO and therefore shared the same fate. Just like him, these prisoners struggled with hell and tried to protect themselves from death. Many of them were broken by such merciless torture and burned alive. But there were also those among them who possessed a strong spirit, steadfastly enduring all suffering and torment. Each of them was tormented by visions of their own misdeeds, and each of them saw the souls they had destroyed as if in reality.

All prisoners of the Sun, through physical suffering, achieved spiritual purification. Unbroken by torture, they gained wisdom. Their deeds were revealed to them in their true light, and they repented of their sins.

Ergos, who once thought himself God, also repented and admitted his guilt. He began to ask SO for forgiveness, but the Creator remained deaf to his pleas. Ergos knew that he would not be forgiven, and he accepted his fate.

Chapter 2 Solar Inferno visions

One day during his imprisonment, Ergos suddenly felt that the temperature of the Sun was beginning to drop. He noticed that it had become much easier for him to cope with the heat. Gradually, he was able to focus his attention not only on fighting gravity and the scorching heat, but also on what was happening around him.

So he soon discovered that many Ota were burning in the Sun, just like himself. They were scattered throughout the solar space.

When Ergos peered into the distance with his superhuman vision, he saw a terrifying sight. Countless Potras had invaded the entire solar system like locusts. On planets with solid surfaces, they installed powerful pumps and extracted energy from the Sun. The dwarf star, which had provided warmth to all living things on Earth for hundreds of millions of years, was doomed.

The Earth itself was also a pitiful sight. There were no forests or rivers left on it. The world's oceans had receded significantly, revealing vast areas that had been hidden under water for thousands of years. Entire cities, once submerged, became visible on the surface. In many places, temples dedicated to Ergos appeared. Long ago, they had miraculously survived the tsunami and been submerged in the sea.

Deserts stretched across almost all continents. Those who miraculously survived hid in caves or ruins of houses. Many of the survivors were held in concentration camps, where they were subjected to brutal torture.

The actions of the Potras reminded Ergos of his own sins. Once upon a time, he himself had been just as ignorant, cruel, and conceited, believing himself to be more powerful than the Creator. "How could SO allow this to happen?" Ergos wondered. "But what business is it of mine? The fate of humans is the concern of the one who created them."

Suddenly, he heard a plea for help coming from Earth. The voice was exactly the same as Rokhan's. "That vision again," Ergos thought bitterly and was already lost in thought when he suddenly heard the voice again. This time, the ultrasonic sound of words in the Yue language begging for help reached him very clearly.

Ergos listened and looked more closely, but he no longer heard the plea for help. Suddenly, he saw a long purple beam half a meter in diameter appear out of nowhere in space and head toward Earth. This beam burned through the Potras' warships on its way and, upon reaching Earth, pierced a massive cluster of black soldiers. Many of them were instantly flattened, while the rest lay on the ground: some without heads, some without legs, some with their torsos burned through.

In the purple beam, he could see the silhouette of a woman bravely fighting countless enemies. Trying to figure out who she was, Ergos listened to her heartbeat and shuddered. From the rhythm and tone of her heartbeat, he realized that this woman was his daughter. His breathing and heartbeat quickened. The news that he had a child stunned him. Trying to calm down, he began to breathe deeply and gradually immersed himself in memories.

Somewhere deep in his memory, he saw himself as the Yellow Emperor, coveting the wife of one of the Kunlun people. Her beauty captivated Ergos. He brought her husband closer to him and endowed him with superpowers. Having become a powerful Ota, the Kunlun man abandoned his wife. The young maiden fell into despair, and Ergos, seizing the moment, began to comfort her and care for her attentively. Touched by his warm words and attention, the girl opened her heart to him and succumbed to temptation. However, Ergos was fickle and soon left her too. When the war between the Ota and the Fundi began, he had already forgotten about her completely.

Chapter 3 En's Final Battle

When the memories faded, Ergos once again began to watch what was happening on Earth. In addition to the purple silhouette of his daughter, he now saw many other glowing silver figures participating in the battle. Ergos recognized them as the Fundi. "I used to be one of them," flashed through his mind.

He wholeheartedly supported the Fundi, grieving deeply over every loss among them. But it was obvious that the Potras were far superior in number, and the Fundi could not overcome such power. Seeing their ranks dwindling, Ergos wanted to help them and tried to fly out of the inferno. But he was unable to do so. The heat and gravitational pull were still too strong. He had no choice but to watch.

The third day of the battle between Fundi and Potras had already begun, and all this time Ergos had been constantly searching for his daughter in the battle and watching her for a long time. She skillfully struck down her enemies one by one, but it was clear that she was already very tired. Potra, on the other hand, seemed to be getting stronger.

After several more days of fighting, the Fundi were completely exhausted. They needed rest in the immaterial world, but the opportunity to move there and regain their strength was extremely rare. As in the battle with Ota, many of the Fundi, not noticing the disappearance of their superpowers in the heat of battle, perished.

En, completely absorbed in the fierce battle, also did not notice how her superpowers began to fade, and soon found herself trapped. This happened when the Potras, during their next attack, suddenly turned into microparticles forming a solid dense ball, surrounding her on all sides.

En attempted to teleport into the immaterial world, but she was unsuccessful. Meanwhile, the sphere began to shrink. Trapped inside, En began to pierce the metal with a laser and ultrasonic waves, but the space inside the sphere was shrinking so rapidly that she was unable to even make a breach.

Realizing she was trapped, En began to scream and cry for help. Responding to her call, the Fundi attempted to break the sphere from the outside, but they were met with a barrage of attacks and gunfire, preventing them from doing so.

The ball continued to shrink all this time. Soon the screams inside it subsided, and agonizing moans could be heard. When the ball had shrunk to the size of a tennis ball, there was dead silence.

Ergos lowered his head. He realized that he had just witnessed the death of his daughter. Tears streamed from his eyes, but they immediately evaporated in the intense heat. His heart was consumed by grief and emptiness. He felt neither anger nor hatred. He no longer cared. Closing his eyes, he willingly ceased to resist the heat and the force of gravity.

Chapter 4 The Ota's emperor enters the battle

After a while, intense pain woke Ergos up. His whole body was engulfed in flames, and he was slowly being pulled toward the center of the sun's core. Instinctively, he began to beat the fire and tried to fly out of the inferno, but after a moment he stopped. "Why?" he asked himself, and was about to close his eyes again and succumb to gravity, but suddenly he heard familiar battle cries.

Looking around, he saw Ota's light brown laser beams, half a meter in diameter, flying out of the Sun and beginning to attack the Potras' ships. On Earth and other planets, he noticed Ota who had already broken out of their confinement and were fiercely fighting the black insectoids.

They too heard the death cry of the girl crushed inside the metal ball. From the beating of her heart, they realized that she was the daughter of their emperor. Although they had long since repented of their sins and accepted their fate, En's terrible death awakened in them a sense of injustice. Loyal to Ergos to the end and sharing his fate, they rushed to punish the murderers of their leader's daughter.

Despite the fact that Ota died solely for the sake of revenge, together with the Fundi, they accomplished many feats, saving their comrades-in-arms and people who had come under enemy fire.

The Kunlun people remained humanity's last hope for salvation, but with every Fundus or Ota that perished, that hope slipped away like sand through their fingers. It gradually became clear that their fight against the Potras was doomed to failure.

Ergos heard the pleas for help from the wounded Fundi. Due to a lack of strength, they could not transport themselves into nothingness to regain their strength, and they were dying. Some of them, with their last breath, managed to turn to SO with a prayer, hoping that He would hear them and come to their rescue.

Fundi's plea reminded Ergos of his daughter's death. He looked once more at the hordes of Potras, confidently and fearlessly destroying the Ota loyal to him, and his eyes burned with hatred. He felt anger, like a long-dormant volcano, begin to awaken within him, filling him with strength. Suddenly, he shot out of the solar inferno with a red laser beam.

Burning through countless hordes of ships, he flew to the place where En had died in a matter of minutes. Landing on the pile of bodies she had defeated, he froze for a moment, his red, motionless silhouette standing out against the backdrop of the general chaos of battle.

At that moment, they started shooting at him. He quickly dodged the shots and let out such an ultrasonic roar that many insectoids instantly turned into smoldering dust. Then he turned back into a red laser beam and flew into the pumping station, which the Potras used to extract energy from the Sun. When he pierced it, flying out the other side, the station exploded.

The blast wave destroyed many of the insectoids and disabled their combat vehicles. The bodies of the insectoids caught in the blast lay on the ground like dead cockroaches after poison. Above them, the silhouettes of Ota and Fundi, who had managed to dodge the blast wave, froze in the air. They didn't understand why the station had exploded and looked around.

Just then, they noticed the silhouette of Ergos. He stood there watching them intently. When they caught his gaze, he greeted them with a brief nod.

Suddenly, a huge black cloud of the Potras began to gather above their heads, and Ergos, instantly transforming into a laser beam, flew into it and began to strike his enemies. Inspired, Ota and Fundi followed his example, and the battle raged with renewed vigor.

In battle, Ergos was cool-headed and calculating. His movements resembled those of an enraged lion pouncing on its prey.

Shooting laser beams from his eyes and emitting a supersonic roar, he destroyed anyone who tried to stop him. He was incredibly fast, maneuvered easily, and deftly dodged shots. Suddenly disappearing and reappearing in another place, he discouraged his enemies and then delivered devastating blows with lightning speed, while remaining invulnerable.

After Ergos entered the battle, the Potras began to suffer enormous losses. This forced them to transfer all their troops, previously distributed between Mercury, Venus, Earth, and Mars, to the battlefield.

So many ships and military vehicles had gathered around Earth that they completely blocked out the sunlight. Everything was plunged into darkness. Only explosions, gunfire, burning combat vehicles and ships, as well as the light emanating from superhumans and their laser blasts, illuminated the battlefield.

Chapter 5 The Battle Between the Super Machine and the Superhuman

It had been six days since the Ota joined the Fundi in their battle against the Potras. The Red Emperor, like his comrades-in-arms, was already severely exhausted. His speed and attention had noticeably decreased.

During another attack by flying Potras, while deflecting shots from laser cannons, he suddenly felt a sharp pain in his back. The blow was so swift that Ergos did not have time to notice it and defend himself. Turning around, he saw the silhouette of a woman hovering a hundred meters away from him.

This maiden was completely naked. She had thick chestnut hair, white skin, beautiful features, and green eyes. Her athletic figure was very reminiscent of an Ota woman: about 180 cm tall, with perfectly proportioned shoulders and hips.

 Ergos initially thought he was facing an Ota woman, but the beating of her heart revealed that she was a cyborg.

It was Jedzala, the queen of all Potras. She alone had the privilege of possessing a natural human appearance. She loved her body so much that she did not want to hide it in spacesuits or armor. On her orders, potra scientists created a unique material that looked and felt just like human skin but was incredibly strong. This allowed her to remain invulnerable without any equipment.

Jedzala strictly ensured that only her body was endowed with the qualities that allowed her to be the most versatile warrior of her multi-trillion-strong horde. She surpassed the other Potras in speed, power, and combat skills.

The queen's body could take on any state of matter: solid, liquid, or gaseous. It could transform into a laser, fire, electricity, or a magnetic-electric storm, completely controlled by her consciousness. Such a body became the pinnacle of scientific achievement, allowing the machine to be in no way inferior to the body of a superhuman.

Against the backdrop of a fierce battle between superhumans and insectoids, a fight broke out between Ergos and Jedzala. They flew rapidly toward each other, exchanging laser shots, which both deftly dodged. When they got close, a hand-to-hand fight began, their bodies transforming into fiery, gaseous, liquid, and laser silhouettes.

They seemed to be mirror images of each other, because their movements were remarkably similar. The fighting techniques they used resembled a mixed style that included elements of kung fu, karate, taekwondo, jiu-jitsu, and boxing.

They moved so fast that the naked eye could only make out two glowing figures colliding and bouncing off each other.

Both were flawless, and only thanks to his ability to anticipate Jedzala's actions, Ergos sometimes managed to injure her. However, any damage to Jedzala's body instantly repaired itself.

The only weakness of this perfect machine was its need for energy. During battle, bubbles filled with Ra energy would periodically fly into it, absorbed by its body like dry soil soaking up life-giving moisture.

The battle between the superhuman and the super machine lasted a very long time. During the battle, Ergos realized that he would not be able to defeat the queen as long as she was receiving Ra energy. Maneuvering and dodging, he began to move imperceptibly toward the queen's large ship, from which energy bubbles were flying out, in order to deprive Jedzala of access to energy.

Jedzala quickly figured out his plan and, using a signaling device built into her brain, ordered her soldiers to strengthen the defenses of her ship. The main forces of the Potras immediately began to converge on that location.

Very soon, a huge swarm of Potras, resembling a swarm of bees, gathered near the royal ship, surrounding Ergos and Jedzala. The bodies of the Potras transformed and merged, forming a giant sphere. Gradually, the sphere began to shrink in size, increasing the density of its walls, and the space inside it began to contract.

Ergos and Jedzala continued to fight inside the sphere. Suddenly, Jedzala flew toward the wall, and her body, turning into liquid metal, merged with the sphere, becoming part of it. Ergos, left alone inside the sphere, realized that he was trapped in the same way as his daughter.

He still had the strength and time to teleport himself outside the sphere, but he decided to put an end to these insectoid monsters once and for all.

EPILOGUE

Inside the shrinking sphere, Ergos' figure, glowing red, assumed the lotus position. He closed his eyes and slowly began to exhale, emitting a soft, melodious sound. It was his prayer to SO, asking Him to save all those who remained alive.

Gradually, his body began to heat up and glow brighter and brighter. When the heat reached its peak, Ergos opened his eyes and said, "I am ready, take my soul."

Immediately after these words, his body exploded. The force of the explosion was so great that the entire spherical structure around him, the royal ship, and many other spaceships instantly evaporated, like snow under the scorching sun.

The shock wave from its explosion swept across all the planets of the solar system, destroying the remaining pumps on Mercury, Venus, and Mars. This was followed by a thick red fog that enveloped everything around it and remained floating in space for a long time.

Ergos perished, but most of the Potras army was destroyed. The remaining Ota and Fundi continued the battle and soon defeated the last of the Potra. At the same time, it was clear that the light brown silhouettes of the Ota first faded and then began to emit a silvery light, similar to the glow of the Fundi. Having finished the battle, the Ota and the Fundi ascended together to another world.

Thanks to the heroic efforts of the Kunlun people, the beating of human hearts can still be heard on this planet, which is now almost uninhabitable. The history of Earth continues, and in the wake of the vanished era of digital technology, a new era will eventually dawn. What will it be like? That is for them, intelligent beings, to decide.

Thank you for reading!

I, Sema Shubekabu, would like to express my sincere gratitude:
To my parents for their love, support, and belief in me.
To everyone who helped me create this book: editors, designers, friends, and inspirers.
To all the readers who open this story and bring it to life.
Without your support and participation, this book would not have been possible.

Sincerely,
Sema Shubekabu